"Do you really want me to stop?"

His words teased, just as his tongue coaxed, circling one nipple.

"Yes," Lanni said quickly. "No! Oh, Chandler," she sighed. "Just love me before I die from needing you."

They were lying together on the bed, arms and legs entangled. His long, muscular thigh parted hers then, and he settled over her with a gentle strength that threatened to overwhelm her.

He kissed her eyelids, the corners of her mouth, and finally deepened the kiss. When he raised his head for breath, desire glittered in his eyes. "Is this what you meant, honey?" he murmured.

Smiling, she moved sinuously beneath him, drawing his lips close once more. "It's a very good start...."

Elizabeth Glenn set this Temptation—
her first one outside her native Texas—in
Michigan, because she admires the state's
great natural beauty. She herself worked
at a summer camp there while in college.
She remembers being fascinated by the
sumptuous residence of the camp's
owners, and wondering what kind of
story there might be in such a place....

Books by Elizabeth Glenn

HARLEQUIN TEMPTATION
124–THE HOMING INSTINCT

HARLEQUIN AMERICAN ROMANCE
14–DARK STAR OF LOVE
36–TASTE OF LOVE

HARLEQUIN SUPERROMANCE
67– WHAT LOVE ENDURES

Where Memories Begin

ELIZABETH GLENN

Harlequin Books

TORONTO • NEW YORK • LONDON
AMSTERDAM • PARIS • SYDNEY • HAMBURG
STOCKHOLM • ATHENS • TOKYO • MILAN

For my two most significant others,
Grim and Doodle

Published October 1987

ISBN 0-373-25275-7

1

THE EARLY JUNE SUN was high in the sky, although the screen of pine and birch trees overhead allowed only occasional brilliant rays of light to penetrate the Michigan woods. Noting the heat, Lanni Mercer Preston feared the hour was closer to noon than ten o'clock. She put her sandaled foot down on the accelerator and urged the battered red Jeep to go faster along the narrow paved road that curved and climbed through the forest then swooped low, as unsettling in places as a roller coaster.

If she hadn't been in such a hurry, Lanni would have relished the drive, the feel of the wind whipping her long, heavy, chestnut-colored hair out behind her, the clean air cooling her damp neck and legs that were bare below denim shorts. She never ceased to be awestruck by the overwhelming natural beauty of Camp Ottawa. As a ten-year-old camper, she had fallen in love with the verdant woods and weathered sand dunes along the eastern shore of Lake Michigan. Something about the place had appealed to the budding artist in her, and she'd been trying to express her admiration one way or another ever since. Even now, nineteen summers later, she would probably drop everything and write an ode to the two bickering squirrels beside the road if she weren't running so far behind schedule that morning.

Her foot pressed down harder as she realized that she couldn't indulge herself. If lunch was late again on her account, she'd . . . she'd . . .

Get over it, a little voice supplied. Lanni grinned. Yes, she'd survive. Even if the entire staff never let her live it down.

As she approached camp headquarters, she heard loud laughter just ahead, around a bend in the road. She removed one slim hand from the steering wheel long enough to rap three warning toots on the horn and slowed the Jeep to take the curve. The crowd of college-age camp staffers tramping along the middle of the road parted to let the Jeep through.

Lanni stepped on the clutch and shifted into neutral, bringing the vehicle to an idling halt in their midst. "John," she called to a lanky redhead, "what time do you have?"

"Eleven forty-five. We're on our way back for lunch."

"Forget your watch again, Lanni?" Teddy Mitchell asked, his expression innocent. "Better put that on your list: sleep in wristwatch so poor hungry staff don't starve."

Shooting a good-natured look at Teddy for his reference to her famous lists, Lanni shifted back into first gear and sped the last hundred yards to the eating lodge, where she parked sloppily. Although she was constantly composing lists of things to do, half the time she couldn't even find the darn list when she needed it. Lanni wasn't known for being organized. The last time she'd forgotten her watch, the camp staff ended up eating peanut butter sandwiches for lunch and had teased her mercilessly ever since.

Luckily the first set of campers wasn't due for another week, but the youthful crew who had arrived early to clean up the campgrounds and buildings all had huge appetites. They needed regular, hearty meals, as the boys frequently reminded Lanni.

She set the hand brake, then vaulted out of the Jeep and ran up the steps of the loading dock to yank open the kitchen door. Inside, the ten staff members she had designated for kitchen duty that week went calmly about their work, too busy to notice her as they put the finishing touches on enough chicken-fried steak, baked potatoes and English peas to feed a small army.

Leaning back against the door, Lanni watched for a moment in puzzlement. How had they prepared a meal without her supervision? This was the way she always hoped they'd be functioning by the time camp started, but in the six years she'd supervised the Camp Ottawa service staff, they'd never managed to do so well so fast.

She straightened in alarm. Maybe they'd forgotten to set the tables! Hurriedly she crossed the room, dodging teenagers who smiled and greeted her when they saw she had returned. She pushed open a swinging door and entered the main eating lodge, an enormous rustic room with windowed walls on three sides, a huge fireplace at the other end and some forty dining tables. Three-fourths of the tables were folded and stacked against the north wall of the room, and the tables that were standing had been set with the plain white crockery and flatware that campers had used for as long as Lanni could remember.

"Praise the Lord, it's a miracle!" she muttered in relief.

"If it is, I engineered it," said an amused male voice. "And you owe me for that, Lanni."

She swung around and found Don Grant, the middle-aged business manager of the camp, sitting at an extra table, grinning at her. He had a ledger book spread open in front of him, and next to the book a calculator trailed a long tape of figures onto the pine floor.

"I'll be sure to add it to my list," she said, strolling over to where he sat.

"*Which* list?" he asked dryly, warm affection in his eyes as he watched her approach.

"The list of favors I owe you," she said and indicated the distance from her shoulder to her fingertips. "It's about this long by now."

"Good. I like having beautiful ladies in my debt." He chuckled when she rolled her eyes at him. Lanni had known him all those years that she'd been a camper there, followed by the four summers she had worked on the linen staff during college. He had told her more than once that the first time he saw the skinny little Lanni Mercer, it hadn't occurred to him that she could mature into such a lovely woman, one whose pensive gray eyes, waist-length brown hair and incredibly long legs would eventually combine to make a striking package. Such a compliment wasn't likely to go to her head, coming as it did from a man who'd been closer to her than a father at times.

Don had pushed for Lanni to fill the position of summer-staff supervisor when it opened up six years ago. She'd been going through a divorce and had felt pretty low at the time, and she wondered now to what extent he'd been motivated by compassion. Certainly he had expected her to do a good job, and she had . . . most of the time.

"Mind if I ask what made you late this time, Lanni?" Don asked good-naturedly.

She held up her bare wrist and shrugged in apology. "Same as before. I was checking out the bath houses at the remote campsite and lost track of time. And you don't have to tell me to put it on my list. Teddy has already done so."

Don laughed again, and Lanni grinned, too, adding, "Listen, Don, thanks for taking over. You saved the day."

"No problem," he said. "To tell you the truth, all I did was remind the kids where the menu was posted, and they did the rest. Most of them have learned about all you can teach them, since they've worked here in past summers. I think it's just as well you don't stand over them every minute. Let them develop a sense of responsibility."

Lanni pivoted to watch as several kitchen workers came through the swinging door bearing platters of food, which they placed on the serving table nearest the door. "They seem to be developing that pretty well," she conceded, "but I wouldn't bet my last dollar that they'll remember on their own to start lunch if I'm late again."

"What the heck." Don stood and slapped his ledger book closed. "It's that uncertainty that makes life interesting." He came around the table and put his arm across Lanni's shoulder in an avuncular hug. He was only slightly taller than her slender five feet nine inches; his sandy hair had become sparser in the past few years, but his body was still firm from playing volleyball and swimming. "That's a quality I enjoy in you, Lanni. I never know what you'll do next."

"What I'll forget to do, you mean," she lamented. They moved to a table near the south windows and sat down, and she nodded at the staff who were gathering just outside in anticipation of the lunch bell. "Teddy jokes about it, but I think he's really terrified that he'll starve to death because of me."

"Ahh...he's a growing boy, obsessed with food. They all are."

"Food and girls, not necessarily in that order."

"Right." Don's smile had vanished, and he was looking out the window, watching someone in the crowd. "Does he seem okay to you?"

"Who? Teddy?" She turned to study the blond youth, who leaned against a signpost beside the driveway, balancing his weight on his right leg. Like the majority of the staff, he was a long-time Ottawa camper who hadn't wanted to give up his Lake Michigan summers when he'd reached the age of eighteen. In the six years Lanni had known him, he had become a favorite of hers. "Well . . . I don't know. It's hard to tell with him, the way he's always kidding around. You know Teddy."

"Yes, I know Teddy." Don frowned for a moment, then shook his head. "Hey, never mind. I'm probably just imagining things. I get the Ottawa jitters this time every year until I adjust to being away from Ruth." He asked Lanni about her family as the bell in the court- yard began to clang and the staff filed into the lodge.

Since Lanni rarely saw her parents in Boston, or her older brother Phillip, a stockbroker on Wall Street, that discussion was brief by necessity. When their table filled up with teenagers, the conversation grew a little rowdy, but she found that infinitely more interesting than fo- cusing on herself or her unremarkable life from Sep- tember through May as a high school art teacher in St. Louis.

It wasn't until everyone finished eating and the kids went back outside that Don got a chance to speak to Lanni alone again. "I meant to tell you, I had a tele- phone call from Philadelphia this morning."

She sat up and took notice of his announcement. Philadelphia meant Scott-Hight Corporation. The Big Shots. Camp Ottawa had been founded in 1920 by Grosvenor Scott for the purpose of helping young peo- ple to develop to their fullest potential. Scott-Hight, a multiinterest company based in Philadelphia, still pro- vided the financial backing for the camp. Numerous underprivileged youngsters from all over the nation received subsidies to the camp sessions each summer, while many well-to-do families paid their children's fees. Executives at Scott-Hight took an active interest in the running of Camp Ottawa, and directives from Philadelphia always received priority.

But that wasn't the reason Lanni's heartbeat suddenly accelerated. For ten years she had been unable to think of Scott-Hight Corporation without automatically remembering Chandler Scott, Jr. It wasn't a pleasant memory.

She tried to act nonchalant. "Oh? And what did Philadelphia have to say to you?"

Don looked pleased and rather excited. "George Wentworth asked us to prepare the Scott cottage. It seems we're going to have company in a day or two."

The slight widening of Lanni's eyes was the only visible sign of her alarm. She furtively wiped her moist palms on her shorts and repeated, "Company?" She wanted to ask if it would be a Scott, but she couldn't seem to make her mouth form the words. Better not to know, anyway. Probably it would just be a member of the board of directors at Scott-Hight, bringing his family for a few days of sun and sailing. After all, there weren't that many Scotts left anymore. Scotty—Joseph Andrew Scott—had died ten years ago, and Chandler, Sr., had died the past October. That only left Mrs. Scott and—Lanni's brain stumbled over the thought—the young Chandler.

Young Chandler? She almost laughed. Ten years ago he'd been young. Now he was thirty-one, two years older than Lanni. Plenty old enough to be married, with an adoring wife, three kids and a dog. And he probably *was* married. She had no reason to suppose his life had been suspended that long-ago summer, just because he'd never come back to camp in all that time.

Nodding, his expression one of preoccupation, Don asked, "Think you can manage?"

"Manage?" she croaked, wondering how Don had known she was positively traumatized at the thought of seeing Chandler again. Did he guess that she had lost her virginity to Chandler Scott in the moonlight on the sandy beach beside Lake Michigan?

"Can you manage to get the cottage ready by to-morrow?"

"Oh!" She slumped in relief. He didn't know! "Oh, sure. I'll get someone on it right away."

Unfortunately it didn't turn out to be that simple. She had already selected her linen crew, the five most dependable girls on the staff who would handle the housekeeping chores all summer, but they were still tied up cleaning the boys' dorm. They had at least another full day's work before it would be ready for occupancy, Lanni estimated, and she considered it essential that the male staff members get moved out of the girls' dorm as quickly as possible. Not that either the males or females were complaining about the overcrowded conditions. They all seemed to be getting along quite harmoniously, in fact, which was just the problem. Some of the friendships were rapidly progressing to the point that close proximity at bedtime offered too much temptation for teenage hormones to resist. Lanni understood the feeling very well.

As for the rest of the staff, she couldn't trust them to bring the Scott cottage to the spit-and-polish perfection that she knew was expected for a visitor from Philadelphia. The kids who would be filling out the kitchen crew once camp started weren't as efficient as the linen crew, and besides, they were busy cleaning guest cottages for the influx of parents. The grounds crew couldn't stand to be confined indoors and so, whether intentionally or not, flubbed every inside job Lanni gave them.

That left just her. She would have to clean the cottage herself. She came to the realization reluctantly as she stood in the deserted linen room and scowled at her clipboard with its lists of jobs to be done before campers arrived. Darn it, why did someone from Scott-Hight have to upset her schedule by coming now? Why couldn't they wait a month? Better yet, why not just stay in Philadelphia where they belonged?

Lanni recognized the tension that was building inside her and fought it. Imagine being afraid of going to an empty house, for heaven's sake. As if an inanimate object would recognize her and . . . what? Point a finger? Laugh? If walls could talk, that big old cottage could more than likely disclose enough conquests by the debauched elder Scott son to fill several X-rated novels. Surely Lanni was mature enough to put the past into perspective and ignore whatever feelings the place stirred up inside her.

At any rate, she had no choice.

FOR A MOMENT after she parked the Jeep under the shade tree, Lanni just sat and stared. The huge log-and-stone cottage was nestled among the pines high on a crest overlooking Lake Michigan on one side and tiny Sandy Lake on the other. Splendid in a rough-hewn way, the house had always held an almost irresistible appeal for her.

Remembering the first time she'd discovered it years ago, she smiled. She had ventured up to the dusty windows to peer in, hoping no one would catch her snooping. It seemed like forever that she had been hearing about the legendary Scotts, who owned the cottage yet rarely spent any time at Camp Ottawa. What a waste, she'd thought as she walked the length of the veranda, identifying each room through the windows as she passed: kitchen, dining room, enclosed sun porch, wide-open library and living area with central stairway that led up to bedrooms and a sleeping porch. There was a big stone fireplace in the dining room and another at each end of the living area. As she peeked inside, Lanni drew a quick mental sketch of the long room during a Michigan winter, lit by blazing fires, with snow piled high against the outer walls and herself wrapped in a warm patchwork quilt, reclining on a sofa and staring dreamily into the flames. After that day, the dreamy feeling had persisted whenever she thought of the great house, until one summer— Lanni broke off her thoughts and climbed out of the Jeep, then reached into the back for her mop, broom, dustpan and bucket packed with cleaning supplies and new rags. If she wanted to get this job over with—and she definitely did—she didn't have time for reminiscences. Unlocking the door beneath the porte cochere, she stepped inside and set her equipment down in the hallway. In the main room she quickly raised half a dozen windows to air out the musty smell, then began pulling off the dusty sheets that covered the solid pine furniture.

Lanni was a fast worker when motivated by something as disturbing as the ghost of a dark young Apollo that seemed to be lurking in every room of the Scott cottage. As she brushed down cobwebs, swept, mopped and dusted, she muttered to herself that she would have been perfectly contented to live out her life without setting foot in this place again.

Then why did you ever come back to Camp Ottawa, a smart-alecky little voice in her head wondered. It wasn't as if she had needed the salary she earned as a staff member. Her parents, after all, weren't exactly hard up.

The simple truth was, Lanni had never been one to take the easy way out. It had hurt her terribly to return to the camp the year after Chandler broke her heart, but she had forced herself to do so. She even took one lonely moonlit walk to the very sand dune where he had sweet-talked her into surrendering to his needs. And every memory that she faced was a little less painful than the previous one, until she no longer felt the deep shame that had once heated her cheeks at the knowledge of what a fool she had been.

Now she no longer hated Chandler Scott with a purple passion. Now she merely felt indifferent to him.

Well, perhaps not indifferent, exactly. Perhaps enlightened distrust was a better way to describe her attitude. Or icy scorn. She tried out several possible terms. Simple distaste. Vehement loathing. Eroding bitterness. Lord, she thought with an unexpected spurt of vengeful energy, she would love to get her hands on that low-down rat!

It was while she scrubbed the kitchen appliances that Lanni's eyes were drawn to the bulletin board on the wall beside the refrigerator. The snapshots thumb-tacked to the cork were old, and she had seen them all before, but now she dropped her sponge and moved closer to study the display. Most of the photographs showed two handsome boys in their teens who had been captured for posterity by a Polaroid. One was tall and muscular, and her stomach somersaulted as she stared at his well-sculpted, olive-skinned face and expressive black eyes. The other was fair and noticeably slighter with a mischievous smile and a pallor that indicated chronic ill health. There were several funny family portraits, obviously posed, with solemn boys and silly, grinning parents. The happiness and affection that the subjects shared was genuine; Lanni had known that the first time she saw the pictures, and everything Chandler had said about his family all those years ago had confirmed it.

Going back to her cleaning tasks, she tried to re-member the name Chandler had used for Scotty's ill-ness...nephritis, she thought it was. A disease that had ruined his kidneys when he was small. Chandler had grown quiet and taut-lipped when he spoke of his younger brother's deteriorating condition, which frightened Lanni into changing the subject. She wanted to hear more about the boy who spent his time in bed composing lyrics and setting them to guitar music, but

Chandler had looked so . . . so *desperate*. It must have absolutely devastated him when Scotty had died.

The sympathy she was suddenly feeling for Chandler annoyed her to no end. "Dadblast it, Lanni," she swore as she pulled the plug in the sink and watched dirty water swirl down the drain, "get your mind on something else!" She hadn't given him this much thought in years, and she understood that it was the cottage's atmosphere doing it to her, making old images seem fresh.

A glance at her wristwatch, which she'd put on after lunch, offered Lanni the excuse she needed to leave. She had to get back to headquarters, to make sure the kitchen crew got supper on the tables by 6:00 p.m. Work in the cottage wasn't finished, as she'd never even made it upstairs, but the rest of it would have to wait until tomorrow.

Although Don sat near her again at supper, the business manager made no further reference to their expected company. After the meal, Lanni decided not to walk to the small resort town of Sandy Lake with the younger staff, who enjoyed hanging out at Perry's Place, the local café. Instead, she grabbed a sketch pad and a box of oil pastels from her room in the girl's dorm and found herself a secluded dune with a view of the sunset. Trying to capture the pink-and-gold magnificence of the sun melting into the water kept her hands as well as her active imagination occupied.

By the next morning, Lanni's muscles were vigorously protesting all her hard work, which led her to the conclusion that she was more out of shape than she had realized. As soon as she saw to it that the staff were all busy at their appointed tasks, Lanni set off on foot for the Scott cottage, glad she had left her cleaning tools there yesterday. Walking would be good limbering-up exercise, and give her a chance to enjoy the nature trail through the woods.

Still in the dark as to who would be using the cottage, she had managed to convince herself that the visitor's identity didn't matter. It could be Chandler Scott and his mistress, for all she cared. She would finish the job, make sure everything was spick-and-span, then go back to her usual supervisory duties and not give another thought to the big shot from Philadelphia. Simple.

Unlike the paved road, the hiking trail approached the Scott cottage from the northwest, depositing Lanni on the long veranda that paralleled Lake Michigan. The kitchen door happened to be closest, so she let herself in through it and gathered her bucket, broom and mop, then headed upstairs.

Thank goodness she had psyched herself up so she had no qualms at all about this place. Otherwise she might have started to wonder why instead of the stuffy air she'd expected to find, she could distinguish a subtle hint of a fragrance that was intriguing, male and very sexy.

Her nostrils twitching, Lanni looked down the hall at all the closed doors. Only the first one stood slightly ajar.

What *was* that scent? Somehow it brought to mind Tom Selleck, which made her shiver and smile. She knew Magnum, P.I. hadn't been here recently. It was just her imagination working overtime.

Propping broom and mop against the wall, she reached out confidently and pushed open that first bedroom door, and the sight of the naked man inside almost caused her to drop the bucket.

2

LANNI STIFLED HER SCREAM with great difficulty, her gray eyes opening wide. *Oh, mercy,* she thought, unable to wrench her gaze from the long, breathtakingly beautiful masculine form that lay sprawled on his stomach across the bed.

Shoulders. Muscles. Cute rear end. Oh, my! Legs. Incredible! Dark. Big.

Jerky, disconnected thoughts and impressions flashed through Lanni's mind during the seconds that she stood there staring. With all her stunned attention focused on what had to be the most superb body she'd ever seen, naked or otherwise, she was scarcely aware that her blood was pounding in her veins, her mouth was dry and her knees weak. She clutched the bucket handle in both hands, her entire being flushed with panicky warmth.

Who was he? The back of his head gave her no answers. But the line of his cheek, the curly black hair, the dark olive skin—and she could see plenty of skin!—seemed tauntingly familiar. If she had to venture a guess, she'd say this was probably the mature version of Chandler Scott, and that Lanni Mercer Preston had just become the victim of one of life's more sadistic practical jokes. The last time she'd seen Chandler, he was wearing the same basic outfit that he had on now . . . nothing! Ten years of overindulged living only seemed to have improved his looks, although she would have to see more to be positive.

As if to accommodate Lanni's unspoken wishes, the man on the bed emitted a soft, satisfied groan and flipped over onto his back before she could look away. And to be perfectly honest, she probably couldn't have made herself look away until she saw all there was to see.

Would you get a load of him!

Heart racing, she moistened her lower lip with the tip of her tongue. Her breathing was quick and shallow, and she consciously tried to slow it down. Heavens above, he was . . . She gulped and swallowed, her usually extensive vocabulary failing her. Who could describe Adonis's assets? Words were entirely inadequate.

Lanni snatched a guilty glance at his upper half and confirmed that he hadn't awakened yet. Also, that her worst fears had come true. This was without a doubt Chandler Scott. She would know that unforgivably handsome face anywhere, although she had never before seen it with the arrogant mouth softened in sleep. He looked downright defenseless. She definitely preferred him this way. If he were to wake up . . .

Lanni flinched in horror at the possibility and began to back up, pulling the door closed as quietly as she could. Her gaze slipped down Chandler's length once more just before the door clicked shut, and she sighed a shade wistfully. *Magnificent muscles,* she thought and ignored the inner voice that mocked her for pretending it was his muscles that fascinated her.

Creeping on tiptoe to the stairs, Lanni carefully set down the bucket, then sank onto the top step. What was she going to do? She had thought she would never see Chandler again. She'd fervently hoped never to see him! No matter how cool and calm she pretended to be about this, she wasn't sure how she would act if it came right down to a confrontation. After all, he had once made a fool of her, and she was human enough to want to forget he existed.

You made a fool of yourself, the irritating voice corrected her.

Impatiently she wiped a sweaty hand down her bare leg. What difference did it make how it was phrased? She dreaded facing that man again. Period.

But that wasn't her only problem. Mental turmoil aside, she had to clean the rooms up here so Mr. Chandler Scott could continue to lie around in the comfort to which he was accustomed, perhaps with his girlfriend or his wife. Maybe another of the bedrooms was occupied, too, although Lanni couldn't imagine him going in for separate beds. For that matter, she thought, as she remembered the way he looked naked, why would any sane woman let him out of her sight?

A hurried inspection of the other bedrooms showed that Chandler was there alone. Lanni peered down at the driveway through the screened windows of the sleeping porch and saw what must be the car he had driven to camp, a late-model blue Buick. Nice, but not exactly the luxury car she would have expected him to select. More than likely it was a rental job. Belatedly Lanni realized that if she had driven the Jeep over today rather than walking, she would have seen the car and known he had arrived, and thus she would have been spared the ordeal of barging in on him. Her pulse rate hadn't yet recovered from the stress of that "ordeal."

Lanni still had to decide whether to clean the empty rooms while Chandler slept, at the risk of disturbing him, or to send over some of her cleaning crew later, when he would, hopefully, be awake. Not to mention dressed.

Did she really want to take a chance on her teenage girls being here alone with that . . . that nude scoundrel? If his seductive skills had kept pace with his good looks, he must rank right up there with Don Juan by now. He'd never exactly been backward in that respect.

No, Lanni was capable of handling Chandler. It was her responsibility to clean the Scott cottage, and she would darn well do it. All by herself.

She used both hands to smooth back several rich brown tendrils that had pulled loose from her ponytail. Rather nervously she tugged down her cropped red-and-white striped T-shirt until it almost met the waistband of her shorts. For some reason she suddenly wished she had dressed a little more conservatively that morning, instead of like one of her teenage workers. People were always telling her she looked about eighteen, anyway, which hadn't bothered her much until that moment.

With a grim determination to get out of there before Chandler woke up, Lanni went to work on the second-floor rooms, making so little noise that one might have supposed her life depended on it. She thought perhaps it did. Her progress was seriously hampered by her fear that if she used the faucet in the upstairs bathroom, the outdated plumbing would wake the dead. It took her a while to carry her mop water a bucket at a time up from the kitchen, but she considered the effort worthwhile.

By the time she'd finished, she had made at least fifteen trips up and down the stairs to dispose of dirty water and get fresh. After repacking the bucket with her cleaning supplies and wearily picking up the rest of her tools, she started toward the stairway.

As she stepped on a throw rug in the middle of the hallway it suddenly shot out from under her feet, sending the bucket, broom and mop in three directions and Lanni in another. The dull thump of her tail-skid landing was lost amid the raucous clatter of an overloaded aluminum bucket hitting the wall and then scattering bottles of Windex and disinfectant all over the floor.

Please. Not this! Tell me I'm dreaming!

CHANDLER THOUGHT AT FIRST he was still dreaming. He'd been having a good dream for once, probably because he was so glad to be back at the camp again, in spite of the memories. Or maybe because of them. He'd spent some of the happiest days of his life at Camp Ottawa, never as a camper, but vacationing with his family.

His family. Even now, the term had the power to hurt, and in order to cover his feelings, he usually spoke the words with a trace of sarcasm. That was a habit he needed to break, if only because he'd had the opportunity lately to see how it made Caroline, his mother, wince. He thought she'd suffered enough.

The ghosts of years past surrounded him here. Everywhere he looked he saw them—Scotty especially, but also his dad. When Chandler had arrived after midnight the night before, having rented a car at the Muskegon airport, he wandered through the rooms for over an hour, absorbing the images like physical blows, as though he had to take his punishment without flinching. Punishment for what, he couldn't say, unless it was that through no fault of his own, he was alive and they were dead.

Despite the pain, Chandler felt no regrets about making this trip. Caroline had been telling him for several months that he needed to get away, and he knew she was right. Running his own company was time consuming enough, but the additional responsibility of serving as chairman of the board at Scott-Hight Corporation, which he'd assumed after the death of Chandler, Sr., was starting to drain him.

Although the bedrooms obviously weren't ready for guests, he'd found a quilt in a closet and spread it over the bare mattress in his old bedroom, then taken a cold shower and gone to bed. Tired as he'd been, he had no trouble sleeping. He'd even dreamed that he and Scotty had taken the *Lady Caroline* for a sail on Sandy Lake. The sun was pleasantly hot on their bodies, and Scotty lay back in the boat, playing his guitar and singing one of his own slow ballads.

All of a sudden Scotty's fluid, haunting music had become a discordant racket that jerked Chandler awake. He sat up in the sun-bright bedroom and stared at the closed door, his ears ringing with the fading echoes of what sounded like a heavy-metal number on a rock radio station. After a moment, there was silence.

Scowling and half asleep, he stumbled out of bed and headed for the door, at the last second glancing down at himself. No telling who was out there. Better not chance it. He grabbed the nearest thing he could see that qualified as clothes—his favorite Levi's, or all that remained of them, a faded, battered pair of cutoffs that he took everywhere and refused to throw away.

Still buttoning the fly with one hand, he opened the door and stepped out into the hall. In fact he almost stepped on the girl who sat on the floor, her slim legs outstretched and an empty bucket lying between her feet. She reminded him of a rag doll, propped up on her arms, head dangling forward.

At first he thought from the way she was dressed that she might possibly be as old as twenty. When she lifted her head and her eyes skipped straight up to the front of his shorts, he revised her age upward by several years. Evidently she had expected him to be naked, and when she realized he wasn't, her expression registered profound relief. Chandler's lips twitched. She had probably looked in on him before he'd awakened and had seen that he slept in the raw. At least, he was pretty sure he hadn't closed the bedroom door when he'd gone to bed last night.

Figuring that turnabout was fair play, he inspected her with a slow thoroughness and liked what he saw. The girl's soft brown hair was pulled back from her face in a ponytail, the severity of the hairstyle relieved by wispy curls that feathered her temples and cheeks. Oval and fineboned, her face was dominated by big gray eyes and a perfect bow mouth. When she met his gaze suddenly, her eyes made him uncomfortable. They seemed to brim with knowledge and accusations that he didn't understand, and yet they were calm, reserved and much more dignified than her position on the floor warranted. Those eyes were a lot older than her face, and he felt an instant kinship with her because of it. Sometimes, he thought, his own eyes must have that ancient look.

Forcing his mind away from that line, he took his time studying the rest of her. She was long and slender. Not as curvaceous as he usually liked, but promising nevertheless. She looked somehow faintly familiar, and he spent a moment trying to place her, without success.

His bold curiosity didn't have the disconcerting effect on her that he'd halfway expected. He saw anger flare up in her eyes before she dropped her long lashes and got to her feet. When she was standing, she looked straight at him again, and he saw that her eyes had grown smoky, unreadable. And very, very lovely, he thought, his stomach tightening in an almost-forgotten way.

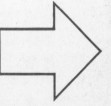

NO COST! NO OBLIGATION!
NO PURCHASE NECESSARY!

PLAY "LUCKY 7"
AND GET AS MANY AS SIX FREE GIFTS...

HOW TO PLAY:

1. With a coin, carefully scratch off the three silver boxes at the right. This makes you eligible to receive one or more free books, and possibly other gifts, depending on what is revealed beneath the scratch-off area.

2. You'll receive brand-new Harlequin Temptation®novels, never before published. When you return this card, we'll send you the books and gifts you qualify for *absolutely free!*

3. And, a month later, we'll send you 4 additional novels to read and enjoy. If you decide to keep them, you'll pay only $2.24 per book, a savings of 26¢ per book. And $2.24 per book is all you pay. There is no charge for shipping and handling. There are no hidden extras.

4. We'll also send you additional free gifts from time to time, as well as our newsletter.

5. You must be completely satisfied, or you may return a shipment of books and cancel at any time.

His reaction irritated him so that he snapped at her. "Who are you?"

Lanni had been about to gather up her equipment for what she hoped would be the last time. At his gruff question, she turned to face him. "I've been cleaning the rooms up here. You arrived before we expected you, or the house would have been ready."

"I can see what you've been doing. I asked who you are."

"I'm Lanni Preston." Would he remember her given name? She hoped not! "I'm sorry if I woke you up. That wasn't my best exit."

He leaned against the doorframe, crossing his arms on his darkly matted chest, his expression relaxing as if he'd been reminded of something pleasant. "You're one of the linen crew?"

Lanni almost laughed. Honestly, the man must think he still had dibs on Camp Ottawa's cleaning maids! "Actually I supervise the entire staff."

Raising both eyebrows, he looked her up and down once more. "How old are you, Lanni?"

"How old are *you*, Chandler?" she countered sweetly.

He hesitated in surprise, then dipped his head in a nod that acknowledged her jab. "I'm thirty-one."

"And I'm twenty-nine."

His dark eyes skimmed over her face, lingered on her mouth as he wondered how it would taste, then slid down to her bustline, which wasn't all that diminutive now that she was standing up. In fact, he liked the way her breasts pushed against the clinging T-shirt. Too bad she wore a bra. The enticing two-inch strip of lightly tanned flesh that spanned the distance between shirt and shorts drew his eyes, leading him to speculate what her skin would feel like. If he placed his palm there to see, what would she do?

From the way he was scrutinizing her, she expected him to say something chauvinistic like, You certainly don't look that old, honey. Instead he asked, "How did you know my name?"

Darn! She had hoped he wouldn't pay any attention to that little slip of hers.

"Oh, everyone knows about you." She knelt to set the bucket upright and hastily stuff the contents back inside.

At her words, Chandler snapped up straight and uncrossed his arms, his mouth thinning with displeasure. A hard knot had just taken form in his stomach. "What are you talking about?"

Lanni stood up, too, her arms full once more. Astonished by the hostility in his tone, she kept a cautious eye on him. "I mean, you're famous around here."

Was he crazy? All the blood seemed to have drained out of his face, and he looked ready to spring, his muscles tight. She began edging toward the staircase, but in a flash he clamped one big hand on her shoulder and stopped her.

"What do you mean, everyone knows about me?"

Stiffening, she demonstrated that her eyes could turn just as icy as his. "Take your hands off me!"

"Answer my question."

He *must* be crazy. And she must have been equally insane to argue with him. "Not until you release me."

It tempted him with its saucy rhythm, and he wondered exactly how it would feel. Now letting go of her slim waist, he squeezed down past her and purposely trailed the fingers of one hand through the smooth strands of hair. *Ahh*, he thought. *Silk!*

When she felt his hand brush her derriere, Lanni's heart jumped. The nerve of him! Fondling her in broad daylight—him practically naked and not the least bit ashamed of it! He hadn't changed at all. If her hands hadn't been full, she probably would have slapped him to kingdom come.

A moment later he stood below her, gallantly relieving her of her burden, and she found herself with no reason not to slap that insufferably handsome face. His glittering black eyes, almost level with hers, focused on her mouth. His sensual lips parted slightly—a devious, underhanded hint for a kiss if she'd ever seen one. At the memory of the kisses he'd stolen ten years ago, she had to clench both hands to keep from going for his throat.

Still staring at her mouth, he heaved an exaggerated sigh of regret, then turned and preceded her the rest of the way down the stairs. Lanni followed him, mentally debating if it was worth the effort to slug him. By the time she reached the bottom, the distracting sight of his bare brown torso and long legs, muscular and well formed, had affected her judgment, not to mention every erogenous region of her body, so that hitting him wasn't exactly uppermost in her mind.

He dumped the tools by the door and held it open for her. "Did you drive over?"

"I walked." She sounded as out of breath as an impressionable teenager, which probably wouldn't help his already overblown ego, darn him!

"I'll drive you back so you won't be late."

"There's no need—"

"Sure there is." His tone brooked no argument. She remembered that willful expression from ten years back, too.

Before she could react, he had escorted her outside and put her firmly into the front seat of the Buick. After rolling down the window for her, he slammed the door and headed back toward the cottage. "Give me a minute."

Did she have a choice?

He returned shortly, dressed in jeans, an oft-washed Harvard sweatshirt with the sleeves cut off just above the elbows, and Topsiders without socks. As soon as he got in and switched on the ignition, she informed him coolly that he shouldn't trouble himself, but he merely raised an eyebrow at her and put the car in reverse. "I told you I was hungry," he said in an injured tone as he shifted into drive. "If you'd been halfway neighborly, you'd have invited me to lunch. I'm just giving you a second chance."

He was giving *her* a second chance! What irony! Lanni opened and closed her mouth without saying a word.

Invite him for lunch? The idea was unthinkable. It was preposterous. It was also insidiously tempting.

After all, she reasoned, she *was* one of the senior staff members, and she had a responsibility—an obligation, really—to be polite and yes, friendly, to the Scotts when they frequented their summer home. Because, she reminded herself, without their help there would be no Camp Ottawa.

Besides that, she wouldn't mind satisfying her curiosity about Chandler. What had he been up to for ten years? What had kept him away from camp? Did he have a wife stashed away back home in Philadelphia?

She turned to face him with a deceptively gracious smile. "By all means, Mr. Scott, you *will* join us for lunch, won't you?"

His answering smile was a trifle arch. "I might be persuaded, if you ask me just right."

"Don't push your luck," she said sweetly, and he tipped back his head and laughed, a deep velvety sound that sent a shiver all the way down to her toes. His teeth gleamed straight and pearly white when he laughed like that, and he looked good enough to— *Stop it*, she ordered herself frantically. When he slowed the car and sent her an inquiring look, she realized she'd spoken aloud.

Embarrassed, she repeated, "Stop. Take me back to the cottage." He stepped on the brake at once, his smile growing wicked. Grimly she added, "I have to get my cleaning things. You left everything sitting by the door."

"Oh, that." He accelerated toward headquarters once more. "It'll still be there when I take you back after lunch."

"Why on earth would I go back?" Did he think she was a glutton for punishment?

"To finish cleaning."

"I've already finished."

"Really?" He cocked a dark eyebrow again in that unbearably confident manner of his, and she could see devils dancing in his beautiful eyes. "Did you clean my bedroom around me while I slept?"

The bright pink flush that suffused Lanni's cheeks announced that she had indeed seen him asleep and naked.

The hardest part for her to endure was Chandler's smug, knowing grin.

3

DURING LUNCH, Lanni frequently felt Chandler's amused eyes on her. She knew very well what he was thinking about when he looked at her, and she could have cheerfully killed him. What was more, each time he let his admiring gaze wander down the front of her T-shirt—which was far too often for her comfort—everyone at the table must have had a pretty good idea what was on his mind.

Then again, maybe they didn't. No one else seemed to notice the erotic tension that crackled between Lanni and Chandler. But, Lord, *she* noticed! Her nerves were singing with it. Her breasts tingled every time those obsidian eyes focused on them, and she was certain the resulting stiffness in her nipples was visible through both bra and shirt. The pit of her stomach swarmed with intoxicated butterflies that fluttered their wings like mad and got nowhere.

Lanni kept sneaking looks at Chandler, only to catch herself picturing him as he had been without a stitch of clothes on his long, hard body. Such imagery didn't exactly contribute to her peace of mind.

Praying the kids were as oblivious as they appeared to be, she struggled to keep her eyes away from the source of her agitation, while listening to the conversation between him and the camp business manager.

"Lanni tells me the cottage wasn't quite ready for you, Chandler. Sorry about that. It's always hectic trying to get everything cleaned up for the beginning of the camping sessions."

"Don't apologize. For once I beat my schedule and arrived somewhere early."

"You fly in from Philadelphia?"

"No, from Dallas."

"Is that right?" Don sounded surprised. "Is Scott-Hight opening an office in Texas?"

"I think not." Chandler hesitated. He'd expected the questions from people like Don, whom he'd known most of his life, but that didn't mean he welcomed them. "I have a business of my own in Mesquite."

"That's right, so you do. Rumor has it you're becoming one of the biggest land developers in the Southwest."

Lanni ventured a curious look at Chandler. She had missed that particular rumor.

"Not the biggest, but the best."

No problem with his *ego*, she thought.

"Looks like you inherited your father's head for business."

Chandler could almost feel the color leave his face at Don's innocent comment. He schooled his features not to react. Friends of the family were always saying things like that to him. They meant no harm. It wouldn't do any good to get up and walk out.

Seeing Chandler's strained expression, Don grew sober. "Listen, I know you miss him. It was a terrible shock when he died so suddenly." The younger man nodded curtly. "How is your mother doing?"

"Fine." He cleared his throat and softened his tone. "Caroline sends you her best."

"You can tell her when you talk to her that I said hello, will you? Why don't you call her from my office tomorrow and suggest that she come out here for a few days."

Chandler made a noncommittal sound and asked the pretty girl on his right to pass the rolls, the only food that hadn't been totally devoured by that time.

"How long are you planning to stay?" Don asked casually, voicing Lanni's thoughts.

Oddly enough, Chandler's eyes slid over to rest on Lanni for a moment before he responded. Her heart pumped faster when she felt his speculative gaze and almost stopped completely when he finally answered. "I don't know yet, Don. Maybe a couple of days. Maybe a month."

A month! Disregarding the risk, she raised her head and stared at him in horror. He couldn't stay a month! Even a week would be dangerously long.

Dark eyes locked with her panic-stricken gray ones and a smile tugged at one corner of his mouth. "Maybe longer," he added with a wink that was just for her. "It all depends."

She could imagine what it depended on. Well, if he expected to be entertained, he was in for a disappointment! She certainly wouldn't cooperate, nor would she

"Why should she have to run it when she has a son like you? Your mother's earned her retirement."

Chandler didn't say anything, and after a minute Don went on. "I'm glad you came back here, too."

Lanni leaned forward until she could see Chandler where he stood with both hands shoved in his pockets, broad shoulders hunched and head bent, the bright sunlight making him more darkly appealing than ever. She could barely hear his quiet, dry response. "So am I . . . I think." He lifted his head then and gave Don a crooked grin. "And I've outgrown your lectures, so let's drop it, hmm?"

Don nodded his agreement. "I know you have, and I'll try, but it may be hard. Every time I look at you, I can't help remembering the mischief you used to get into when you were a kid. You and Scotty."

Chandler's smile slipped a little, and Lanni thought she saw a shadow of pain flicker across his sun-bronzed face. It was obvious that he still missed his brother.

What was all that Don had been saying about Chandler's returning to Scott-Hight after ten years? Where had he gone? Ten years ago he'd just graduated with honors from Harvard with a degree in business administration and had been ready to assume an executive position with his father's huge corporation. Something drastic must have happened to change his plans. Maybe Chandler, Sr., had decided his elder son should start at the bottom and learn the business; the arrogant young man Lanni had been so smitten with wouldn't have liked the idea of working his way up. His experience had taught him that all the good things in life should be delivered to him by first-class express on a silver platter. But could he have been rebellious enough to depart from the family fold?

Chandler turned just then and saw Lanni watching him, and some vital part of him quickened, banishing his unhappy past. She was lovely, with her long soft hair and her thoughtful eyes...although those eyes did seem to take him apart inch by inch as if she were trying to read him. He didn't want *anyone* to know him all that well.

Still, he was intrigued by the hot vibrations that kept shooting back and forth between the two of them, a means of communicating something very physical without words. At lunch, he'd enjoyed the potent excitement of sitting across the table from her, steeping his senses in her slightly tousled beauty and the occasional wafts of her fragrance that drifted over to him. The resistance flaring in her eyes had told him that his presence was every bit as disturbing to her as her nearness was to him.

And they would be alone together at the cottage in just a few minutes.

Anticipation brightened his mood. "I'll see you later, Don. Thanks for the office key."

"You're welcome. The telephone's available whenever you need it."

With a departing wave at Don, Chandler approached Lanni. "You ready?"

She stood and picked up the folded stack of clean linen that she had gathered for him to use at the cottage. "I'm ready, but it makes more sense for me to drive the Jeep over."

"Not when I happen to be going that way." He opened the car door, took the sheets and towels from her and put them in the back seat.

"Yes, but I have to come back this way afterward."

"So do I. Don invited me to supper, in case you've forgotten."

Fat chance of that! She gave him a disdainful look as she climbed in, and when he had gotten in and started the engine, she said, "It's five hours until supper. It won't take me more than half an hour to clean your bedroom."

"Good. That leaves us four and a half hours to do . . . mmm . . . other things."

His suggestive words and the gleam in his eyes stimulated a hunger that Lanni usually kept subdued. Traitorous feminine needs began to make themselves known to her, and she fidgeted.

For heaven's sake, she was having crazy thoughts again! He was not some knight in shining armor, someone who would enrich her life by cherishing her forever. If she gave him half a chance, he would love her and leave her—it was a simple as that. It was up to Lanni to protect herself, because Chandler Scott had no scruples about using people. She'd already learned that the hard way.

Feeling the liquid fire spread through her bloodstream as she remembered how he had looked in bed, she feared she hadn't learned her lesson all that well.

"Tell me, Chandler," she asked with a direct gray stare, "exactly what 'other things' did you have in mind to keep us occupied after I finish cleaning your bedroom?"

"Ahh . . . I thought maybe we could spend some time getting to know each other a little better."

Her eyes were doing it to him again—dissecting him with a kind of cool disgust that puzzled him. How could he receive such powerful signals of desire from her one minute and the next instant see what appeared to be active dislike in her eyes, her face, her very posture?

"I think we know each other about as well as necessary," she said, turning to face the front and putting an end to the discussion.

Fine, Chandler thought in annoyance. *Just fine.*

When they reached the cottage, she hurried upstairs, while he threw himself down on one of the sofas in the living area to gaze moodily out the nearest window. He felt as bleak and empty as the vast gray stretch of Lake Michigan that formed the distant horizon.

Well, he'd asked for this rejection. How stupid could he get—feeding her that line about wanting to get to know her better. He knew damn well he wouldn't let her or anyone else get close enough to really know him. She'd probably seen through his ruse and wasn't interested in playing games. Actually he didn't need the games, either. It had been different when he was younger, but at his age he'd long since stopped enjoying the challenge of making a woman fall in love with him.

It would be so much better, he thought, to be honest. To just tell her the plain unvarnished truth—*I need you. You look so warm and touchable, I can hardly keep my hands off you. I want to make love with you. We can do a lot for each other.*

Without really planning to, he rose and climbed the stairs, then stood for a moment in the doorway of his bedroom, watching Lanni wash one of the four big windows. Her face was averted, but he knew she knew he was there. The tilt of her head looked stubborn; the curve of her cheek and the slender line of her body made her seem vulnerable. For some reason, both traits appealed to him, and he had another impulse to make an honest request: *Hold me, Lanni. Lie down with me and put your arms around my waist and hang on tight. I want to feel your warmth, your softness and strength. I want the comfort of being with you. That's all. No sex. Just two people touching, sharing, caring about each other for a little while.*

He clenched his jaw at the thought of saying anything like that. He'd never even recognized such a need before, although he suspected it had been growing deep inside him for a very long time, for as long as he'd been alone. For ten years, to be exact. The women he'd allowed himself to know during that time hadn't been ones he might be tempted to care about.

Still not sure what was driving him, Chandler crossed the room to Lanni's side, ripped several paper towels from the dwindling roll and sprayed a fine mist of window cleaner onto the dirty pane of glass that she hadn't yet got around to. Quickly and efficiently, he wiped the window until it shone, then proceeded to clean the dresser mirror.

If she hadn't been trying so hard to remain aloof, Lanni would have stopped what she was doing to gaze at Chandler in complete astonishment. His actions couldn't have surprised her more if he'd rubbed the Windex bottle and produced a genie that did windows.

While she swept the floor, he took the bucket to the bathroom and brought it back full of water, then began mopping as if he had more than a passing acquaintance with that humble task. By the time Lanni had dusted the furniture, he had finished the floor, so that when she flipped open the fitted sheet and spread it over the mattress, it seemed only natural for him to help her make the bed. Neither of them spoke as they worked, but her mind was racing, processing this new information about Chandler Scott. He was remarkably handy to have around, she thought. Where had he learned these domestic skills? She studied him furtively, wishing he didn't look so breath-catchingly handsome and so . . . so misunderstood!

All right, maybe she *had* been unfair to him. Maybe he'd changed. Lord knows, his body had improved, if that was possible for someone who had been a perfect '10' all his life.

Watching him tuck in his corners neatly, she couldn't help staring at his hands. Strange that she hadn't noticed when he touched her, but he had calluses. His hands, big and strong looking, bore several small white scars on both sides, in stark contrast to his olive skin, and the palms definitely were callused. Although the nails were well cared for, his hands looked as if they'd done their share of hard manual labor in the past. They didn't look as if they ought to belong to someone who'd been raised in the lap of luxury.

Lanni acknowledged to herself with growing confusion that she *liked* those hands. They made him seem human.

When they had each slipped a pillowcase over a pillow and dropped them in place at the head of the bed, Lanni swallowed a sizeable lump of pride. "Thanks for helping."

"You're welcome." Chandler wandered over to look out the corner window at the silver shards of sunlight glinting on Lake Michigan, barely visible through the pine trees.

"I forgot to bring curtains," she apologized. "I can walk over to the linen room and get them...."

"Don't bother." He swung back to face her, his eyes reserved. "I like it better without."

"Well... if you're sure." She hesitated to say more, knowing that after her earlier rudeness she had no business asking questions, but she couldn't seem to help herself. "You know you're really pretty good with a mop. I was, uh, surprised."

He hooked his thumbs through a couple of belt loops and leaned one hip against the dresser. "No kidding." His voice was dry and a little cool.

"No kidding." Curiosity pushed her. "Where'd you pick up that kind of experience?"

"I got my own place when I was twenty-one. It was a long time before I could afford to hire a housekeeper." He shrugged. "It was either clean up after my-self or live in filth."

Her eyes widened at what she was hearing. Chandler Scott, Jr., hadn't been able to afford something? The heir to millions? She'd read that Chandler, Sr.'s enormous estate had been almost equally divided between his wife and his son, and she found it hard to believe the elder Scotts would ever have withheld anything that Chandler asked, even if they had quarreled.

"Well, I think it's terrific that you learned to clean house," she finally overcame her amazement enough to say. "Your wife probably considers you a real jewel."

A mocking light stole into his black eyes. "If I had a wife, I would certainly hope it wasn't my housekeeping abilities that impressed her."

Lanni's eyes were drawn as if magnetized to the front of his snug-fitting jeans. "You don't need to worry about *that*," she said with irony, then glanced up and met his gaze with a blush of chagrin. "Oh, Lord!" She bit her lip. "I've got to go now."

Hastily she packed the supplies back into the bucket and looked around for the rest of her tools. Out of the corner of her eye she saw Chandler coming nearer, but she did her best to ignore him. When he reached out with his callused hands and caught both her wrists, then turned her toward him, she felt her resistance slipping.

He pulled her up against him, thigh to thigh, and settled his hands on her slim waist to hold her still. The way they were standing, she could feel every muscle, every angle, every contour of his supremely masculine body where it fitted against hers. Her skin absorbed his heat while nerves from her breasts to her knees were bombarded with heavenly sensations.

"I want to talk to you," he said.

His musky scent filled her nostrils, a hundred times stronger and even more enticing than that first sexy whiff of him she had discovered in the hallway that morning.

"T-Talk?" she gasped, her pulse leaping.

Nodding, he looked down at her with smoldering dark eyes that burned over her dew-soft skin like a fevered caress, then lowered his head until their lips met. "But first, I want to kiss you."

His mouth was rough one second, silky the next. It tasted fresh and clean and felt like the dreams she'd had for years. Spirals of pleasure twisted through her, searching out every last nerve ending in her body to be sure she knew who was kissing her. And she did know that much, even if every other scrap of reason had deserted her. Caught up in the magic of his kiss, Lanni experienced a dizzying sweep of feelings that left her more than a little confused.

When she put her arms around his neck, his hands slid up under the cropped-off hem of her T-shirt. His thumbs traced over the tender flesh beneath her breasts and elicited a soft moan from deep in her throat.

He nuzzled along her jaw to her ear, then sighed. "I've been wanting to do that since I first saw you."

Did he mean since he first saw her today, or ten years ago? Lanni blinked up at him as she tried to formulate the question.

"You wanted it, too, didn't you?" he asked huskily.

"I didn't think so, but...oh, Chandler, you're *good!*" Too dazed to realize what she'd just admitted, she combed her fingers through the glossy black hair on the nape of his neck and savored the silky thickness.

"You're not bad yourself." His startlingly white smile made her heart flip over.

"Am I better than I was at nineteen?"

He focused on her mouth, thinking how perfect it was, while something stirred again at the edges of his memory, a very faint impression of someone he'd kissed a long, long time ago.

But that girl had been nothing like Lanni...had she? He relegated the memory to the back of his mind with an appreciative chuckle. "Lady, you couldn't possibly have kissed that well at nineteen."

She didn't really want him to connect her with the naive young innocent she had been, did she? Shouldn't she be relieved that he'd forgotten?

Lord, she thought, as the mesmerizing movement of his fingertips on her midriff continued, a person could get drunk on the sensations he was evoking so effortlessly. The last of her willpower seemed to be melting from his heat.

Chandler captured one of her hands and carried it beneath his sweatshirt, cupping it against his ribs. His heart racing, he acknowledged that he didn't want to examine too closely the reasons for this explosive reaction to a woman. For ten years he'd been careful not to let himself care too much . . . about anyone. Surely it was safer just to enjoy the exhilarating present, the heady feel of her against him. His arms circled her waist again as he whispered, "Hold me, Lanni. That's it, use both hands."

Despite the euphoric state brought on by his languorous caresses, she began to wonder why he was slowly edging her toward the newly made-up bed, murmuring compliments in her ear. "Mmm, nice! Lord help me, that's beautiful. *You're* beautiful." His voice was husky, soft. "I can't believe how good it feels to touch you, sweetheart." Yes, she thought. Oh, yes! It felt good, especially when he planted a feathery kiss on her earlobe. "I promise you, you're going to enjoy this, too."

As his meaning finally registered, Lanni dug in her heels and refused to budge another inch.

"You make me wish I had come back here years ago. If I'd known you were here, nothing could have kept me away." His hands were sliding persuasively along her spine. "Ahh, Lanni, don't fight what's happening. Just relax. I would never hurt you."

For a minute there, she'd almost thought he remembered her. A shaft of fury lanced through her, and she pushed his arms away as if his touch burned. "A bastard like you doesn't worry about who gets hurt."

Chandler's head snapped back. "What did you call me?"

"A bastard." Her eyes flashed with contempt so that she didn't notice the quickly veiled anguish in his. "I know your type. Rich, spoiled playboy. You think you can take whatever you want just because you happen to have the right name."

His chest constricting, he jammed his hands in the pockets of his jeans and turned away abruptly to try to steady his breathing. "Leave my name out of this. What happened here has nothing to do with who I am."

She probably ought to keep her mouth shut if she didn't want to find herself without summer employment, but Lanni's simmering resentment was too hot to ignore. "I disagree. I think, Mr. Chandler Scott, that if you hadn't grown up believing you were better than ninety-nine and nine-tenths percent of the population, you might not be operating today under such a blatant misconception."

By now he had swung around to watch her again, his expression closed. "What misconception?"

"The notion that you're bestowing a huge favor on a woman when you proposition her."

He frowned impatiently. "Did I mention sex?"

"I doubt if it's ever necessary for you to mention sex, but it amounts to the same thing. 'Come on, Lanni, let's go to bed. I'm good.'"

His frown became a sardonic smile. "You're getting it backward, aren't you? You're the one who told me I'm good. All I said was, you would enjoy it. For all you know, I might have been after your stimulating conversation."

That stopped Lanni. *Had* she said he was good? She sputtered impotently for a moment, wishing she could deny his claim, yet remembering that she had indeed used those very words to him just minutes before.

She had to settle for giving a haughty sniff. "Believe me, Mr. Scott, I have no desire to find out if you're good in bed."

Some honest-to-goodness humor crept into his smile. "Interesting paradox, Lanni. You body seems to send out a very different message when I touch you."

Lanni shot him a withering glare as she headed for the door. "Dream on, buster."

She was halfway down the stairs when his parting taunt reached her. "When you decide to start being honest with yourself, you know where you can find me."

"Don't hold your breath," she muttered, taking out her frustration on the door as she slammed it shut behind her.

4

SHE SHOULD HAVE KNOWN BETTER than to hope Chandler would take his appetite elsewhere at suppertime. At a quarter to six, Lanni glanced out the south windows of the eating lodge and narrowed her eyes at the sight of the dark and infuriatingly handsome man who strolled over from the administration building, dwarfing Don Grant who walked beside him. Even from a distance, she could see that Chandler was armed with his usual surfeit of assurance. The episode with Lanni at the cottage had evidently not disturbed him.

Well, why should it? If one lady turned him down, he no doubt had his choice of a dozen others. In fact, it wouldn't surprise Lanni if she was a minority of one who had ever said no to Mr. Scott.

"Omigosh," Penny Phillips mumbled, startling Lanni out of her trance. She turned and found the small blond college freshman standing next to her, staring out the window. "He's smashing, isn't he?"

Lanni didn't need to ask who she meant. Penny's eyes were fixed with reverent awe on Lanni's nemesis.

"Oh, yes. Smashing," she echoed, thinking that she wouldn't mind smashing a mop over his egotistical head.

"All that and rich, too," Penny said with a lusty sigh before she returned to the job of setting the tables.

Lanni's mood was a shade cantankerous as the staff trooped into the dining hall. When Don motioned her over to sit with him and Chandler, she pretended not to notice. Within seconds, every empty place at his table had been taken by simpering teenage girls, Lanni saw, to her disgust.

All but one of the linen crew had succumbed to the temptation. Well, at least Denise Sharp appeared to have a level head on her shoulders. Lanni took a seat across from her and asked, "How'd it go at the boys' dorm today?"

"We finished cleaning it at three minutes to five," Denise answered, not sounding altogether thrilled at the accomplishment. As John Bedford and Teddy Mitchell pulled out chairs beside Lanni and sat, she guessed why. Denise didn't want the guys to move to the opposite side of camp.

"Hear that, fellows?" Lanni asked. "You're getting your privacy back. No more curling irons in the sink and waiting in line for the bathroom."

"Thank heaven!" Teddy said with exaggerated enthusiasm. "I can't tell you how tired I am of girls parading around in sexy nightgowns. I've been losing a lot of sleep at night."

"Yeah, all those long beautiful legs. Very distracting." John shook his head in mock disapproval.

Their foolishness almost lifted her spirits. Lanni grinned as she said, "After supper we'll help you move into your own dorm."

"Tonight?" Everyone at the table protested in unison.

"Couldn't it wait until tomorrow, Lanni?" Denise asked. "We're supposed to finish our volleyball tournament this evening."

"Moving won't take long." Lanni would feel a lot more in control once the males and females were separated at bedtime. Jack Mills, a twenty-three-year-old graduate student who worked on the grounds crew, would do an excellent job of chaperoning the boys, she knew.

When the kids failed to talk her into delaying the move, the topic of conversation shifted, and as they ate, Lanni's thoughts wandered to that table across the room. What was Chandler saying that had Don laughing and all the girls looking both delighted and slightly scandalized? It would be just like him to reminisce about his youthful amours in order to entertain at dinner.

The very idea set her teeth on edge. Lanni stood up, gray eyes glinting, and rapped her silverware against her nearly empty plate, calling for attention. Chandler's table was the last to quiet down. Everyone looked at Lanni expectantly.

"Since the linen crew finished preparing the boys' dorm today, we're going to move the guys over immediately following supper." Not surprisingly, her announcement was greeted by groans and loud lamentations. "If everybody helps, you'll still have plenty of time for volleyball afterward."

"Who cares about volleyball?" a boy shouted, clutching at his heart. "I don't want to move!"

Lanni ignored the noisy laughter. "I'll see you all at the girls' dorm in half an hour," she said, then swept out of the dining hall without so much as a glance at the person responsible for her foul mood.

Because of the crowded facilities, everyone had been living out of trunks for the week and a half that they'd been at Camp Ottawa, and it didn't take long for the boys to cram their scattered belongings inside and latch the lids. Lanni saw the camp truck, kept scrupulously clean by the grounds crew between garbage-hauling missions, back up to the porch of the girls' dorm, a two-storied redwood lodge situated in a tree-shaded hollow behind a dune that faced Lake Michigan.

"Okay, folks, our ride's here," she called, and within minutes the large truck bed was loaded down with college students and gear. Lanni opened the passenger door, jumped up on the running board shouting, "Everybody in?" and scrambled into the cab as the truck began to roll.

To her horror she discovered that the driver was not Jack Mills, as she had expected.

"You!" she hissed in disgust.

"Me," Chandler Scott agreed with a lazy grin that he must have known was virtually dynamite. He leaned across the front seat and pulled the door shut to prevent her from falling out. Although she tried to flatten herself against the ancient vinyl upholstery, his muscular shoulder grazed her nipples and his scent enveloped her, setting off a chain reaction of erotic impulses in her body. She felt as if she'd just grasped a frayed electrical cord and was receiving a series of small, highly stimulating jolts that rocketed straight to her toes.

The instant Chandler straightened, she grabbed for the door handle. "What are you doing here?"

He took his foot all the way off the brake, and the truck shot forward at a speed that guaranteed Lanni would stay put. She had no desire to break her neck.

"I'm just following orders," he said, keeping his eyes on the road as it curved past the eating lodge and linen room. His olive-skinned callused hands held the steering wheel with a relaxed strength that had some sort of grip on Lanni's heart.

"Whose orders?" she snapped.

"Yours. You said, and I quote, 'I'll see you all at the girls' dorm in half an hour.'"

She gritted her teeth. "You knew very well I wasn't talking to you!"

"How was I supposed to know that? You didn't say, 'I'll see everyone but Chandler at the girls' dorm.'"

Crossing her arms on her chest, she turned her head away in hopes that not seeing her chauffeur would make her less acutely aware of his magnetic presence. If only he didn't smell so darned good! If only his masculine heat didn't fill the cab and almost permeate her skin . . .

"Are you trying to tell me that if I was handing out orders to you, you'd obey?" she asked, clearly not buying that notion.

"Within reason."

"Ha!"

He glanced at her then briefly, curiously. "Why should you doubt what I say?"

"Because you aren't the type to take orders."

Chandler thought about that a moment. "Considering that it's been less than twelve hours since we met," he said softly, "I hardly think you're qualified to make judgments about me."

Oh, if he only knew! Lanni pursed her lips and kept silent, but her jutting chin conveyed her anger during the rest of the short ride. How dearly she would love to tell him just exactly what she knew about his character, or lack of it.

When they arrived at the boys' dorm, near the entrance to Camp Ottawa, Chandler parked the truck within a few yards of the front door. Energetic bodies began spilling out immediately, reaching back to help others. Chandler climbed down from the driver's seat and strode to the rear, where he took charge with an ease that illustrated what Lanni had just said about him.

She had to concede, though, that he put his muscles to good use even as he issued commands, taking hold of both handles of a trunk to swing it off the truck bed, grabbing two suitcases at a time and then distributing them to staff to be carried inside.

She watched for a moment, reaching the conclusion that she was redundant there. Perhaps she should have been making sure everyone's luggage ended up in the right room.

But inside the dorm, she saw that the boys were better organized than she had given them credit for. Good friends had quickly teamed up to room together and were in the process of selecting the rooms they wanted.

Red-haired John Bedford beckoned Teddy from a door halfway down the hall. "Hey, Ted, I put your trunk in here."

"So that's where it got off to," Teddy said, picking up his jammed-full laundry bag and slinging it over his shoulder. "I thought someone had swiped my stuff." He staggered toward John, complaining about the weight of his burden.

Lanni recognized that Teddy was using the situation to camouflage the slight limp he'd had since he was twelve years old. The first year he'd been at camp, she had overheard him answering the candid questions of other campers who wondered why his left leg was so undependable. Whenever he'd tried to run, the leg buckled.

The boy had informed them casually that his leg was still a little weak from having been in a cast for nine months. He had broken it falling off a horse. Not just any horse, but one of his father's finest Thoroughbred race horses. Teddy confessed that he had been riding bareback, against orders, but after the mishap his father had been too concerned to scold Teddy. "He brought me candy and games in the hospital," the youngster had told his audience. "And when I got home, he'd bought me a brand new model railroad, with farms and villages and mountains all over the place. I could control the trains from a panel of switches beside my bed."

At the time Lanni had wondered if Mr. Mitchell's excessive indulgence might have stemmed from guilt feelings at having provided inadequate supervision of his son. Teddy's parents were divorced, and the boy never mentioned his mother. That must have been some fall, she thought, because no simple fracture would take nine months to heal. She'd guessed from the surgical scars on Teddy's knee and ankle that he had several pins holding the leg together.

As if the kid hadn't had enough of being laid up, the next year he'd arrived for his three-week camp session sporting a cast on his right arm. "Don't tell me you've been riding bareback again," one of his chums had said. Teddy had just laughed and said he'd broken his arm roller-skating. In view of his unsteady left leg, his answer surprised no one.

In the years since then, Lanni had noticed that the always-anxious-to-please camper with curly blond hair and blue eyes often played the role of clown, using humor to cover the fact that his leg still bothered him at times. Not once in all the time she'd known him had she ever heard him complain—at least, she thought dryly, not about his personal problems. He had been known, however, to set up a loud hue and cry if the camp menu didn't feature hamburgers at least twice a week, or if lunch was five minutes late. It was a wonder the kid didn't weigh three hundred pounds.

After Lanni carried the last of Teddy's suitcases to his and John's room, she checked to make sure all the other male staff members were satisfied with their sleeping arrangements. Not quite ready to deal with Chandler again, she emerged from the last room reluctantly. But whether she was ready or not, there he was, leaning one hip against the open front door, regarding her with speculative black eyes.

What was going through his mind? It was impossible to tell his thoughts. Hers, on the other hand, must have been etched in red across her flushed cheeks. Did he intend to kiss her again? How could she get the message across that she wanted nothing to do with him without seeming any ruder than she'd already been that afternoon at the cottage? After all, he was a big shot around there, and he could have had her fired in a minute.

As the teenagers drifted out into the hall, leaving their unpacking for later, she spoke brightly. "I'm sure Mr. Scott has better things to do than wait around for us. If you want a ride back to the beach, get in the truck now."

"We've decided to walk to Perry's Place and hang out awhile," Denise informed her.

"But . . . your volleyball tournament!" she protested.

"It'll wait till tomorrow. Why don't you and Mr. Scott come with us?"

"I can't," she said too quickly. "I have to write a letter."

Chandler was looking at her knowingly, his beautifully shaped mouth very nearly smirking. "I'm going your way, so I'll drive you, Lanni."

"I can walk—"

"Don't be silly. I'll drive."

And that was that. He took Lanni's arm with what looked like gallant courtesy, but she knew better than to think she could shake off his firm grip. As he handed her into the cab, she steeled herself mentally for a wrestling match. If he got fresh, she'd give him a karate chop in the Adam's apple. She'd even hit him below the belt if necessary. Anything to escape.

To her surprise, he didn't touch her on the drive back. He didn't even speak. He hummed softly beneath his breath, a song that was high on the current country-and-western charts, and his velvet voice did a tricky number on Lanni's heartstrings. By the time he delivered her to the girls' dorm and sat there watching her with amusement lurking in his dark eyes, she was experiencing a wildly irrational wish that he *would* kiss her.

But as he made no move toward her, Lanni opened her door and slid down off the high seat, wishing the butterflies in her stomach would just fly away. "Thanks for the ride," she said a trifle hoarsely.

"I'll be seeing you, Lanni."

It sounded like a threat, a warning. It was almost certainly a promise, softly spoken and tinged with humor. Damn the man! No doubt he sensed the way she couldn't help reacting to him.

Lanni didn't mean to waste a moment thinking about such a conceited charmer. Sometimes, however, even the noblest of intentions can't discipline the subconscious mind. Her dreams that night featured a Latin-dark lover who spoke with a cross between an Ivy League accent and a Texas drawl. It could be no one else but Chandler Scott. The dreams tantalized, to say the least. They also irritated her when she woke up and remembered them in vivid detail.

If she had run into Chandler at breakfast that morning, she'd have had a hard time being civil, even to the board chairman at Scott-Hight. Luckily he didn't come to breakfast.

Or lunch.

By suppertime, she was exhausted from looking over her shoulder all day, half expecting him to pop up out of nowhere and pounce on her. When she realized that he wasn't going to show up for supper, either, she lapsed into a mood that, if she didn't know better, would seem to be one of disappointment.

After the dining hall had been cleaned up and the kitchen crew dismissed, Lanni took her paperback novel out on the upstairs deck of the girls' dorm to catch the fading rays of the sun, but she found it no easier to concentrate on reading that night than the night before. Maybe the book was boring. Maybe she was letting herself be distracted by the shouts and laughter from the volleyball game underway on the beach nearby. Maybe it was the missing VIP who had seduced her mind away from the plot. Where *was* Chandler, anyway? Why had he stayed out of sight all day? Had he perhaps left Camp Ottawa and gone back to Dallas?

She let the pages of her book flutter closed, gazing restlessly at the colorful western sky over the lake. It wouldn't get dark for at least another hour yet. She could take a walk as far as the Scott cottage and see if the rented Buick was still there. If it wasn't, she could quit worrying, secure in the knowledge that Chandler had vanished from her life again.

She didn't stop to consider what she would do if the car *was* there. Tossing the book on her narrow bunk in her bedroom downstairs, she donned a pair of sneakers, then slung a red cardigan over her shoulders and tied the sleeves around her neck. Her khaki walking shorts and white cotton blouse might leave her chilly as dusk approached.

Lanni hadn't progressed very far along the beach before the sparkling lake proved an irresistible temptation. Removing her shoes, she walked through the sand at the water's edge. The sensations that accompanied going barefoot were linked with a thousand memories from her childhood and teen years. The gritty texture that tickled the soles of her feet, the sand oozing between her toes, the cold water lapping around her ankles carried Lanni back to her first cookout on the beach, her first night spent out under the stars, and memories of her favorite counselor who didn't laugh when Lanni went to bed clutching her ancient teddy bear.

Lost in the past, Lanni strolled along without looking for landmarks. She didn't notice when she passed the giant twin dunes with the solitary pine shooting up between them. That tree should have alerted her that she had nearly reached the trail that led from the lake up to the Scott cottage far above.

Another thing she almost didn't notice was the big dark man in white swim trunks who lay stretched out flat on his back on the beach, just above the tide line. She had nearly splashed her way past him when she happened to glance to her left. There he lay, to all appearances sound asleep.

She halted, inhaling sharply. Oh, no! Not again! This was the limit. She absolutely could not let him find her there, gawking at him as if she were some wide-eyed innocent who'd never seen the likes of him. She had seen the likes—twice, as a matter of fact. Naked, even. With a loud gulp, she realized that except for a few skimpy inches of taut white cloth, which contrasted dramatically with the dark tone of his skin, she would be seeing him naked for the third time right this very minute.

Thank goodness he believes in swim trunks, even if he doesn't go in for pajamas, she thought fervently as something warm and pleasant stirred in the pit of her stomach.

A regretful sigh whispered through her parted lips, and she pivoted on one foot to backtrack along the lake's edge before Chandler had a chance to discover her. She stepped carefully, lifting each foot high and then putting it down in such a manner as to prevent noisy splashing. The exaggerated stealth must have made her look like a caricature of a Scotland Yard detective, creeping along in pursuit of clues. She should have been carrying a magnifying glass rather than her tennis shoes.

The thought made her giggle, but an instant later her laughter choked off abruptly when she heard Chandler Scott's voice, low and husky with sleep. "There you are, Lanni. I've been wondering when you'd come back to see me."

5

WITH AN UNCONSCIOUS GRIMACE, Lanni turned and met Chandler's gaze. He had propped himself up on one elbow and bent the opposite knee, and he lay there looking like a *Playgirl* centerfold. Given his picturesque surroundings and the fact that he was dressed for swimming, he'd have made a stunning model for a full-color brochure to be distributed by the Michigan tourist bureau.

"I didn't come back to see you," she said.

Chandler didn't believe her halfhearted denial, but he decided not to argue with Lanni this time. Let her keep up her little pretense of indifference if it made her feel better.

Seeing the faint smile Chandler wore, Lanni said coolly, "Actually, I thought you might have left camp, since you didn't show up at the eating lodge today." Her tone implied that the idea hadn't exactly bothered her.

Chandler rose to his feet in one lithe movement and stretched, easing the tightness out of muscles that had been subjected to very little exercise that day. He gave his broad shoulders one final rippling shrug and reached down for the blanket on which he'd lain. As he shook the sand off it, he said conversationally, "Sorry to disappoint you, but as you can see I'm still here."

Darn it all, why couldn't she remember that this man must expect to be treated with absolute respect by virtue of his position?

"I'm not disappointed to find you here." Her polite words drew no more than an arching of one black eyebrow and a slight widening of his cynical smile. She knotted her hands into fists and tried again. "I was just surprised."

He folded the blanket over the crook of one arm, murmuring, "Uh-huh."

"*Honestly.*" Suddenly it seemed very important to her that he believe she wanted him to enjoy his stay there. She had a responsibility to Don—to the entire camp foundation, not to mention the kids who benefited from coming here—not to alienate the man who controlled the purse strings. "You must be awfully hungry by now."

Chandler thought about the hunger that had gnawed at him relentlessly in his dreams and had intensified ever since he'd awakened to find the lovely, chestnut-haired nymph trying to sneak away without being discovered. She was, he figured, talking about a different hunger.

His stomach chose that moment to growl, and he laughed at the timing. Surprise flitted across Lanni's delicate features and then she laughed, too, a hesitant, musical and totally enchanting sound. Chandler's chest constricted with an errant stab of that other hunger.

"Ahh . . . yes. It wouldn't do me much good to deny it, hmm?" he asked, his voice slightly hoarse.

Lanni's knees felt like rubber. His soft, throaty laughter had affected her like a blow to the solar plexus, and she wanted to hear more of it. She was dangerously attracted by his natural charm and his sun-heated skin, and it took all her willpower not to reach out and touch him.

Breathlessly she said, "If you'll come back to the kitchen with me, I'll fix dinner for you." It was the least she could do, she reasoned sanctimoniously.

"There's no need to trouble yourself, but thanks for offering." He squinted his eyes and looked beyond Lanni at the huge orange fireball balancing on the horizon. Even as he stared, his expression rapt, the molten gold of the water seemed to absorb the sun, sucking it lower inch by inch. A trace of something deceptively young and wistful appeared briefly in his eyes and tugged at her heartstrings before he released his breath in a quiet sigh. "Some things never change. Thank God." Shifting his gaze a couple of inches, he focused on her face and said, as if she hadn't almost seen into his soul, "I could use a cold beer right now. How about you?"

A cold beer would be too fantastic for words, but their chances of finding one thereabouts were probably nil. Camp Ottawa had strict rules forbidding alcoholic beverages on the premises.

"Iced tea would be nice," Lanni said, noting how parched her mouth was from her long walk.

"I believe I can fix you up," Chandler said agreeably, hitching up the lagging end of his blanket and then setting off up the path toward the Scott cottage.

If he'd applied even the slightest hint of pressure to make her come with him, she would have resisted with every ounce of strength she possessed. But he didn't even glance back over his shoulder to see if she was following him. He hadn't touched her at all, she reminded herself. And she *was* thirsty.

Still clutching her tennis shoes in one hand, Lanni scampered up the steep side of the sand dune after Chandler and when she reached the veranda, entered through the kitchen door, which he'd left open behind him. He was already putting ice in a glass, and after filling it up from a big jar labeled Sun Tea, he handed it to Lanni and took an icy Coors can from the refrigerator.

Her shocked expression as he popped open the tab made him chuckle. He drank a long, satisfying draft, lowered the can and ran the back of his wrist across his mouth, his eyes sparkling. "I did offer you one, remember?"

She nodded, struck anew by his resemblance to the handsome puckish teenager in the snapshots on the wall nearby. Rules were made for ordinary people, not for the Chandler Scotts of the world. He could charm his way out of anything...or into anything, she corrected, thinking uneasily of her heart.

Taking a sip of her tea and wishing it were a beer, she avoided looking at him, afraid of what his state of undress would do to her already-vacillating pulse.

"You've been shopping," she observed, seeing a variety of canned goods on the cabinet shelves.

"I have, indeed." Chandler opened the refrigerator again and removed a foil-covered platter and two sealed plastic bowls. "Leftovers from my lunch," he explained as he set them on the table. Stripping off foil and lids, he revealed enough barbecued chicken, potato salad and cole slaw to turn Teddy Mitchell green with envy.

He hesitated as he reached for the dinner plates and glanced at her questioningly. "Did you say you're hungry?"

She suddenly became aware that she wouldn't mind having a snack. She didn't think she should admit it, though. There was something so . . . so intimate about the idea of sharing Chandler's leftovers, even though he was waiting for her answer in a perfectly disinterested way, as if it didn't matter to him whether or not she joined him for supper. He hardly had anything on, a fact that her eyes confirmed for the fifteenth time by dipping below his shoulders and slipping all the way down his olive-skinned length, then darting back up to relative safety.

"I . . . er, no, I'm fine."

Just then her own stomach rumbled, and Chandler lifted both eyebrows in mocking disbelief. He put two plates and napkins on the table and got out silverware from the drawer. Sitting down at one of the place settings, he gestured casually at the other. "Just in case you change your mind."

Feeling a little foolish, she ended up taking a seat across from him and helping herself.

So *that* was the way to handle her, Chandler mused. She wouldn't tolerate being pushed. He'd suspected as much from his first contact with her, but he'd been too stubborn to change his tactics. It had thrown him off balance to recognize how badly he wanted to handle Lanni successfully, and he had fought the impulse. It had been so damn long since he'd felt the need to seek out the company of one person in particular. He wasn't sure he liked the feeling, even after ten years of settling for quantity in place of quality. There was a certain numb safety, after all, in large numbers of anonymous female bodies.

On the other hand, there was no use denying that Lanni was good for him. By some miracle, just having her here helped neutralize the anguish that seemed to taint these rooms for him. She distracted him from thoughts of Scotty and his parents, which was no small feat in this house. None of the other women he'd known could have accomplished that. Still, he had no intention of telling her what she did for him.

"This is very good," she said between bites, and he accepted the compliment with a modest smile. "Where'd you pick up this skill?"

As a matter of fact, he'd learned to cook at the same time he developed his other domestic talents—when he was working his tail off in the oil fields of West Texas. Socking away every dime he could spare, saving against the day when Solo Enterprises would become a reality, he hadn't been able to afford to eat out. Of course, anyone having knowledge of the Scott family assets would find that difficult to believe.

"Here and there," he answered, standing up to get another beer out of the fridge. This time when he offered one to Lanni, she declined with sincere regret. She could hardly expect the staff to respect the rules if she returned to the dorm with beer on her breath.

"It has a flavor of Texas," she said of the barbecue sauce.

Chandler nodded. "You should have met the old geezer who taught me the basics. Sam was a relic from a chuck wagon if I ever saw one. It wouldn't surprise me if he'd cooked for the last of the great cattle drives. I ate red beans and cornbread for a year before he got around to trusting me with his recipes for chili and barbecue sauce."

Lanni stared in surprise. Was he serious? He certainly didn't look as if he were joking. In fact, when he glanced up and saw the astonishment on her face, he seemed to regret having said so much.

His mouth tightened. Chandler seldom confided in people. He would never have mentioned old Sam Tucker, nor for that matter anything about that period in his own past, if he'd thought it would make Lanni regard him as a curiosity. Not that he was ashamed of anything he'd had to do. It was just that people who thought they knew all about his connection to Scott-Hight might understandably wonder at the hard times he'd chosen to endure, and he had no wish to open himself up to questions.

Lanni was indeed wondering, as she'd done when he demonstrated his proficiency with a mop. The Chandler Scott who had starred in her earliest romantic fantasies wouldn't have dreamed of learning either cooking or cleaning skills, nor had he been interested in fraternizing with "old geezers." He'd been perfectly happy limiting his contacts to his social peers. She was beginning to suspect that Chandler had changed far more than she'd given him credit for yesterday.

"Sam sounds like an original character," she said. "How did you happen to meet him?"

There was a wealth of genuine interest in Lanni's voice and in her wide gray eyes, and it transfused a subtle warmth into Chandler's bloodstream. A dangerous warmth, he realized at once, as it spread through his taut limbs and made him ache for more. Before she could disarm him completely, he steeled himself to make the only choice he could make. No one must get close enough to know the real Chandler Scott.

Lanni felt a wall develop between them as clearly as if it had been a physical thing. His eyes, just moments before dark and alive with images of his friend, grew opaque, as if a veil had dropped in front of them.

"We worked together," he said evenly.

"Not for Scott-Hight," she guessed, her expression quizzically amused. Scott-Hight probably had very few old geezers on the payroll.

His lips gave a reluctant twitch, but he only said, "No."

"Did he work for you after you started your development company?"

"No."

This was something like pulling teeth, she thought. "You knew him before that?"

"Yes."

Frustrated, Lanni realized that he didn't plan to volunteer a thing. She'd have to dig if she wanted information. She took out her mental tools and started digging. "I was really surprised to hear Don mention that you only recently went to work for your family's company."

His voice chilled noticeably. "I can't imagine why that should interest you."

"As I told you before, you're famous around here. I've spent my summers at Camp Ottawa long enough to have known from the time I was a kid that Chandler Scott, Jr., was the heir apparent to the Scott-Hight throne. Naturally I assumed that you'd made your father happy and joined the family firm a long time ago."

She figured out within seconds that she'd said the wrong thing. His face went rigid, he compressed his lips, and every muscle in his powerful body seemed to coil tight with potentially volatile energy.

After one long, strained minute, his throat relaxed enough so he could speak. "I feel sorry for you, lady. You must lead a helluva boring life if you have nothing better to do than speculate about the activities of someone you don't even know."

Lanni's breath caught. He'd obviously wanted to hurt her with that cold, superior put-down, and he'd succeeded. Not just because her life was boring, although no doubt by his worldly standards it was frightfully so. The worst of her pain radiated from the small, hidden, not-quite-healed sore that had festered in her heart all this time. She'd wasted more time than she cared to think about wondering what had become of Chandler. A man who didn't even remember that he'd known her, she thought in disgust. Well, she darn sure didn't need him to point out the shortcomings of her existence.

"You're absolutely right," she said, standing up and crossing to the door with calm dignity. "Even so, I believe I prefer my boring rut to your company any day."

She didn't bother slamming the door this time, and he didn't fire a parting round at her. Jaw clenched, he remained seated for a long time after her controlled departure, regretting the way he'd lashed out at a woman whose only mistake had been to comment on a situation that puzzled her.

Leaning his elbows on the table, Chandler grasped his head between both hands. He threaded his fingers through thick, curly black hair that had always been as startlingly different from Scotty's and his parents' blondness as night and day, and rubbed his scalp in an effort to ward off the beginnings of a headache.

Fool, he chided himself. *Why'd you have to let her get to you like that?*

With a deep sigh, he acknowledged that the problem had gone beyond his usual anguished reaction to the topic of his family. Now he also had to contend with his guilt over having senselessly hurt Lanni. The startled pain that he'd seen in her gray eyes would probably keep him awake all night.

He was starting to suspect Lanni Preston had been seriously burned by some man in her past. To his discomfort, he wondered if he reminded her of that man. It might explain her instantaneous mistrust of him.

What he'd *really* like to have explained was why he cared so damn much that she mistrusted him.

LANNI WAS HALFWAY BACK to the girls' dorm before she realized she'd left her tennis shoes on the floor just inside Chandler's kitchen door. She felt her blood pressure rise and her temperature zoom past the boiling point. Damn, damn, damn! Fate must be conspiring to destroy her peace of mind.

Well, her shoes could just sit there and rot for all she cared. He could throw them out with the garbage. It wouldn't be the first pair he'd cost her. She wouldn't go back to that place for all the gold in Beverly Hills. She'd had it with Chandler Scott!

The next morning, she left Denise and Jack in charge of the staff and borrowed Don's car to drive to Muskegon with the excuse that she needed to pick up some supplies. After completing her necessary shopping in the city, she stopped by the Muskegon Museum of Art to view the traveling Smithsonian exhibit that was currently booked there, then picked up some crackers, cheese and fruit at a supermarket and went to the P. J. Hoffmaster State Park for a picnic. For a long time she'd intended to visit the Gillette Nature Center at Hoffmaster, so after eating she did so. The story of Lake Michigan's natural development, presented in displays and slide shows, fascinated her.

All in all, the day spent away from Camp Ottawa gave her plenty of time to think, and she returned to Sandy Lake in an improved frame of mind, arriving a few minutes after six o'clock.

Everyone had already sat down to supper when she entered the eating lodge, and the tables all seemed to be full. Don Grant waved and called her name above the clamor of voices, indicating that he was making room for her next to him, so she threaded her way to his side. Only then did she see Chandler was seated across from Don.

Lanni assessed Chandler as warily as he was looking at her. From his slightly tousled, finger-combed hair and the ever-darkening tone of his skin, she guessed he'd spent the afternoon napping on the beach again. When she caught herself studying his sunbronzed face with genuine concern, wondering if he would ever catch up on all the sleep he needed, she dragged her gaze away. Neither of them spoke to the other, although everyone else at the table greeted Lanni with high spirits.

"Have a good trip?" Don asked as she sat down.

"What he means is, did you make it back without wrecking his car?" Teddy interpreted.

Nodding, Lanni handed Don his car keys and began filling her plate, although her appetite had just deserted her.

"We finished every job on your list today, Lanni," Denise informed her.

"So did the grounds crew," John said.

"That's good." For the life of her, Lanni couldn't remember a single item on the work agenda she'd posted in the linen room before leaving that morning.

"Yeah, we cleaned the cages and everything, just like you told us," Teddy said with a sidelong wink at Denise, which Lanni missed.

"Oh . . . great. That's fine," she mumbled distractedly, wishing Chandler would avert his eyes. What did that oblique look mean?

Don looked up with a start. "Cages? Cages for what?"

"Elephants," Teddy answered solemnly at the same moment that Denise said, "Bears."

Elephants and bears? Lanni gaped at her staff in sudden bewilderment, only to flush when she heard Chandler's deep laughter mingle with Don's and the teenagers'.

"Just checking to see if you were paying attention, Lanni," Teddy apologized with a penitent grin.

She shook her head at him in exasperation, even though she knew perfectly well that he wasn't the cause of her embarrassment. "Teddy Mitchell, your jokes are going to be my undoing one of these days! I ought to put you on the next bus to Kentucky."

"I don't think his father would appreciate that," John said in a voice of somber warning. "Summer's the only time he gets a vacation from Ted and his perverted sense of humor. You wouldn't want to be responsible for Mr. Mitchell's throwing a fit and canceling his donations to the camp fund, would you, Lanni?"

"Heavens, no! How would I ever explain that to the board of directors at Scott-Hight?" She allowed a trace of sarcasm to sharpen her question, glancing at Chandler as she did so.

The board chairman seemed not to have heard her taunt. His dark gaze rested on Teddy, while Teddy's eyes were fixed on his plate, his face for once inanimate.

Lanni studied Teddy with concern, wondering what could be troubling him. A moment later she decided she must have imagined his stricken expression because he was smiling at something Denise was whispering in his ear. Thank goodness! Lanni wouldn't want to think she had hurt him with her teasing threats to send him packing.

Seeing Chandler's eyes shift once or twice to Teddy as they continued eating, Lanni tried to figure out what could be of such interest to the man, but his face was unreadable. It was clear, however, that Don at least was worried about the boy, because he drew Teddy into a discussion of the registered quarter horse his father had given him that spring.

Teddy assured them that his father had tried to talk him out of spending the summer in Michigan. "He'll probably fly up to see me in July," Teddy informed them casually.

John looked skeptical. "How come he never made it to Parents' Weekend once in all the years we were campers?"

"Things always came up at the wrong time."

"Well, it seems to me that if he was as anxious to come as you say he is, he'd find a way to put off other things."

"That's not always possible. You can't put off horses." Teddy's voice rose. "Damn you, John, you don't know my father, so don't go telling me how he should act!"

For a second Lanni feared there was going to be a fight between the two good friends. She could feel Don's tension. Even more strongly she sensed the alert attention of the dark man across the table. Everyone else sat in astonishment, unable to grasp the fact that Teddy was angry. Teddy never lost his temper!

But after a highly charged thirty seconds, John dropped his eyes and apologized in a subdued voice. "Sorry. You're right—I've never met your father."

"So just keep your mouth shut about him."

John nodded.

Supper ended on a grim note, and as soon as possible Teddy escaped, followed closely by Denise. In a minute only the three adults and John remained.

By then the red-haired youth was looking both guilty and sullen. He stood up and glared at Don, then Lanni. "His father's a jerk. I don't have to meet him to know that much. He can give Ted a hundred horses, but that doesn't mean he cares anything about him." Turning, he stomped out of the dining hall.

The business manager sighed heavily and got to his feet. "Guess I'll go pour oil on troubled waters."

"Would you like me to come with you?" Lanni asked, not certain what she could say to make things better. For a long time she'd had her own doubts about Mr. Mitchell's effectiveness as a father.

"No, let me see what I can do," Don said.

Lanni nodded and shut her eyes, rubbing her forehead with one hand, her elbow propped on the table. Lord, she was tired! It had been a long day.

"Welcome back," Chandler said softly.

6

THE VELVET MURMUR, laced with irony, sent a shiver of apprehension ricocheting through Lanni. For a couple of minutes she'd actually forgotten that the head of Scott-Hight Corporation still sat across from her, watching the boys' skirmish from start to finish. It couldn't have given him a very positive impression of Lanni's staff-management skills.

Cautiously she lifted her head and looked at Chandler. He stared back at her contemplatively, as though waiting for her to set the tone of their exchange. "I beg your pardon?" she said.

"After spending the day in the normal world, you must feel like you just tumbled down the rabbit hole."

She took a deep breath, relieved that he hadn't criticized her—or anyone else—for the argument he'd witnessed. "I could say the same about you." Her slim hand made a sweeping gesture to indicate their surroundings. "This is probably a bit of a culture shock for you."

A frown line appeared between his dark, arching eyebrows, then smoothed itself out. "You mean because I haven't been back in ten years?" He shook his head. "I spent so much time here with my family when I was a kid, I couldn't forget the place if I tried."

Alarm raced along Lanni's nerves. The last thing she wanted to do was bring up that subject. One thing she'd accomplished that day was to reach the understanding that Chandler Scott's apparent problem had nothing to do with Lanni and everything to do with his family. She hadn't a clue as to the nature of the conflict, but the past three days had shown her proof of his tendency to overreact whenever the topic arose. Last night he'd taken his emotional hang-ups out on her, and she had no desire to repeat the experience.

While she was trying to come up with a safe response, he glanced restlessly around at the kitchen crew who were cleaning off the tables. In a couple of minutes the workers would reach this side of the room, and all hope of privacy would be lost. He'd spent half the day composing an apology—a first for him—and he didn't intend to offer it in front of an audience.

Standing abruptly, he circled the table and took her arm. "Come with me, Lanni."

His palm was warm and rough on her skin, his callused fingers strong. Unexpected and undeniably pleasurable impulses began to radiate out from a core of heat at the bottom of her stomach, connected in some intrinsic way to his firm grip on her arm. The idea of resisting him occurred to her, but she dismissed it at once without questioning why.

A moment later, Chandler escorted her out into the sunshine on the porch of the eating lodge. Still holding her arm, he paused and looked forward where the paved road curved past the girls' dorm to dead end on the beach. From there his narrowed gaze slid to the left and focused on the blue Buick parked in front of the administration building. In the space of a few heartbeats, he considered his options and reached a decision. "We're going for a ride."

Spoken like a true chairman of the board, she thought. Imperious. Arrogant. Confident of her acquiescence. Well, for once he was right. She felt too achingly soft and alive inside to disagree with him.

"Any particular reason?" she asked as he hustled her in that direction.

He could think of several reasons. Just her delicate fragrance and the lovely, vulnerable way she looked in her ice-blue cotton sundress were enough to make him wish he could steal her away to that little inn on the Gulf of Mexico, down near Palacios, Texas.

"I want to talk to you," he said, giving the most innocuous of his reasons.

Oddly, Lanni found that every bit as disturbing as a declaration of passionate intent would have been. She'd had enough experience with would-be Romeos to know how to respond to overzealous advances. But what in the world could they possibly have to talk about?

Relax, she told herself grimly as Chandler opened the car door for her. He wasn't likely to fire her. Why should he, when he could get Don Grant to do his dirty work?

The only possible other topic that she could think of was the time they had known each other ten years ago. Could he have finally remembered?

Leaning back against the comfortable upholstery, she reasoned that it would be far better to get things out in the open than for her to go on holding them inside, resenting, remembering....

It had been a summer evening very much like this one, except that it was in the middle of August. The Michigan countryside had been as green and lush then as it was now, the road through Sandy Lake as narrow, shaded by tall pine trees at this time of day. During the week that Chandler spent alone at his family's cottage, he'd noticed the shy Lanni Mercer for the first time and had charmed her into sneaking away from the staff lodge each day after supper. Together they zoomed along this highway in his red Porsche, the top down, her long hair billowing.

Back in those days, except for staff outings, leaving camp was frowned upon, as Chandler had been very well aware. It was the first time Lanni had ever broken the rules; she'd never had such a tempting reason to be disobedient before. But Chandler Scott exhilarated her. With him she felt daring and unconventional and sexy. It was amazing how a little illicit romance could suddenly make her see that she was a grown woman and had been for some time, even if she wasn't usually treated like one.

They had talked for hours, sitting in the parked car or on the beach. Actually Chandler had done most of the talking, thinking out loud, as it were, about the position awaiting him at Scott-Hight. Several times, though, his confident pose had slipped and he revealed a gnawing concern for his younger brother, who was very ill at their home in Philadelphia. Chandler thought his parents had sent him to Michigan to protect him, so he wouldn't see how bad things were becoming. She knew he feared that Scotty was going to die. Feeling very tender and grown-up, she did her best to reassure Chandler that everything would be fine. All her defenses fell when she saw the melancholy in his eyes. She would have done anything in the world to cheer him up.

That, in part, explained why she was so amenable to his wishes. With the wind whipping through Lanni's chestnut mane and ruffling Chandler's luxuriant black curls, they had driven each evening past miles of cherry orchards and summer cottages to New Era, where he bought them sodas at the old-fashioned ice-cream parlor on the town's main street. Just before curfew, he whisked her back to the dorm and kissed her goodnight with a thoroughness that should have alerted her.

Poor kid, she thought, remembering her innocence. She had sat at the table with Chandler every day that week, drowning in the liquid darkness of his eyes, reading so much more into those looks than he ever said. He didn't have to say a word when his eyes conveyed such flattery, such promise. Their hands touched under the table, and his fingers melted her skin to the bone.

On his fifth night at camp, instead of driving to town, he suggested that they go for a walk on the beach. "Take off your shoes," he urged her, already barefoot himself, brown and strong, exuding youthful virility.

Half a mile down the shoreline, he dropped her sandals in the wet sand, took her in his arms and began a very effective assault on her senses. His mouth and hands played on her body with practiced skill, reducing her to a mass of throbbing desire. When they finally broke apart and walked on, she left her shoes behind.

By the time she remembered them, everything had changed for her. She had followed the instincts of her heart and given everything that the dark young god asked of her. He had asked for and taken everything without hesitation. His husky, lingering "Good night" when he walked her back to the dorm was murmured with regret. "You're beautiful, Mercer," he whispered, holding her close again as though he hated to let her go. "I wish you could stay at the cottage with me."

"That would be wonderful," she agreed.

"I have a little influence around here. Maybe I could arrange it with Don."

"Don't you dare!" she gasped, horrified at the idea of the camp business manager finding out what had been going on. But when she looked up at Chandler's face in the shadows where they stood, she saw the devilish glints in his eyes and she knew he was teasing her. "Oh . . . you! I never know when you're serious."

"I'm never serious."

How true those words had been! Of course, by then it was too late to matter, anyway. Lanni was in love, and she had risked her self-respect on the basis of that love, while Chandler had risked nothing, lost nothing.

"My sandals," she moaned, looking down at her sandy feet. "I forgot them."

"I'll buy you a dozen pairs." He planted a kiss on the end of her small, straight nose. "I'll take you to Muskegon tomorrow and buy you the entire shoe store."

So much for promises. The next day he was gone. He didn't say goodbye, didn't leave a message for her, didn't come back to resume their relationship a day, or a week, or a month later. Don Grant probably would have made an excuse for Chandler's hurried departure, but Don himself had to leave for a week when his wife underwent an emergency appendectomy. By the time the business manager returned, summer was virtually over and it was time for the staff to go home. Besides, by then Lanni had smothered her hurt in pride and wouldn't have asked about Chandler to save her soul. Not even during the terrible five days when her period was late and she was bleakly—and, thank God, erroneously—convinced she was pregnant.

She had never asked about him and as a result had heard very little about Chandler over the years. Once in a blue moon, one of the senior camp counselors, who'd put in as many summers at Camp Ottawa as Lanni, would comment that it had been a long time since young Chandler had been there, and everyone would agree that it had been a while. Someone else would then tell a yarn about the elder Scott son and his wild but utterly irresistible ways. Lanni never took part in those reminiscences, but she couldn't keep herself from listening avidly, hoping for news about Chandler.

IT WAS CRAZY, she thought now, for her to be sitting there in a car beside the man who'd disillusioned her so thoroughly ten years ago that she'd never been able to discuss him with anyone. It just proved she was as big a fool as she had ever been. He was the one who'd changed, who was hard and rude where he'd once been happy-go-lucky. Only his sex appeal remained the same. The man emanated sheer animal magnetism, a potent masculine aura that pulled at Lanni in spite of the deep roots of her shame and anger. No matter what her mood, he made her think of entwined arms and legs, of passion-dampened skin, of breath-catching, dark-of-night, clandestine rendezvous. No matter how hostile he acted, he still had the power to make her want him.

Glancing at him in annoyance, she noted his brooding expression. The Chandler Scott she'd once known would never have scowled like that.

"Well?" she snapped. "Let's have it."

His dark eyes jumped over to inspect her face. "What?"

"I presume you have something to say, so why don't you just spit it out? I don't have all day."

Her irritable outburst probably would have amused him under other circumstances. She had remained docile for all of ten minutes. As it was, it convinced him that his apology couldn't come a moment too soon. He wished he was better at humbling himself. "I guess I owe you an apology."

As his grumbled words sank in, Lanni wondered if her hearing was suddenly failing her. Could he actually be apologizing for the way he'd used her and then vanished without a word ten years ago? And in that reluctant, half-sulky tone, as if he resented being held accountable?

She crossed her arms on her chest and sniffed. "It's high time you admitted it."

He should have known she wouldn't take this very graciously. He shot her an annoyed look. "You're the one who hid out in Muskegon all day. I guess maybe you think I should have tracked you down last night?"

"Last night?" Lanni was beginning to suspect that he wasn't apologizing for the same thing she was blaming him for. She turned to look at him at the same time that he reached over into the back seat and retrieved her scruffy-looking tennis shoes.

"Yours, I believe," he said, handing them to her.

She accepted them with a sense of confusion that rapidly settled into a hard knot of bitterness in her heart. He still didn't remember the way he'd hurt her, dammit! "You're apologizing for last night?"

Nodding, he faced the road again. "I think you probably took what I said the wrong way."

She clenched her jaw. "I doubt that."

This woman really needed a lesson in accepting apologies, he thought ruefully. "Okay, maybe I wasn't exactly tactful."

"You were rude and insulting."

He winced, then heaved a deep sigh. "I guess I was. I'm sorry."

"And in the future, you might keep in mind that not every female on earth gives a hoot whether you think she's boring."

"I never said—"

"Or that you find their life-styles pitifully dull. After all, not all of us can afford to treat the world as our own personal playground."

Chandler shook his head impatiently. "When I made that crack, I wasn't thinking of you. I didn't mean to slur your life-style, Lanni. I was in a rotten mood."

"Are you ever in any other kind?" To heck with playing it safe. She wanted answers! "You know, I've noticed this time around that you get on your high horse every time someone mentions your family. Either that or you change the subject, or clam up, or something just as devious."

They had arrived at the little town of New Era, and Chandler slowed down to accommodate the speed limit.

"You've noticed 'this time around,'" he repeated, scanning the storefronts as he drove along. "That sounds as if we'd met before."

How could she have let that slip out—"this time around"!

"Well...naturally we met," she admitted faintly. "I've spent most of my summers here." She had to come up with a diversion! "What on earth are you looking for?"

"I just found it," he said, parking along the curb. Lanni looked up at the ice-cream parlor and felt her heart sink slowly to her knees as he added, "This place has the best hot fudge sundaes in Michigan."

She knew that only too well. Why did he have to bring her *here*?

Inside, they sat on swivel stools at the counter. Seeing the once-over Chandler got from the young lady who worked there, Lanni remembered that he'd inspired the same admiration in the clerk ten years ago.

Nothing had changed. Chandler still didn't notice the effect he had on the girl. His mind was elsewhere. He didn't especially like the way his apology had gone over, but then he'd never had much experience at that sort of thing. Better leave well enough alone, he guessed. Besides, there were other matters he wanted to take up with Lanni. "What can you tell me about Guy Mitchell's son?" he asked.

"Guy Mitchell?" Lanni had to think a minute. "Oh, you mean Teddy?"

Her interest piqued, she loosened up at once. It would have surprised her to know that her gray eyes began to glow and her mouth softened into a warm, kissable smile. She looked, Chandler thought, incredibly sweet. He knew the sweetness was something she allowed herself to exhibit only fleetingly. Most of the time she armed herself with a thinly veiled anger that seemed to be directed straight at him for some reason, to his increasing dissatisfaction.

Which was the real Lanni Preston? And why was it becoming so important to him to draw her out of hiding?

"What do you want to know about Teddy?" she asked.

"Have you known him long?"

"As long as he's been coming to Camp Ottawa. Six years. He's the kind of kid who gets close to everyone."

Close to everyone? Up to a point. But Chandler was willing to bet the boy had never really opened up to anyone in his life. His laughing mask covered something. For just a second at supper, Chandler had gotten a glimpse of what lay behind the mask.

"Listen, if you're worried about the way Teddy jumped on John, you can rest assured they don't have a problem. They've been good friends for a long time. This one little argument won't change that."

She spoke firmly, as if she would personally and single-handedly shield the youth from Chandler's intervention. He wondered what it would take to get her on *his* side like that.

"Teddy's a terrific boy," she continued fiercely.

Chandler held up a hand. "Okay, you've convinced me. Teddy stays." There had never been any question of that, but she probably wouldn't believe him if he told her so. He accepted the nut-encrusted ice cream cone that the girl handed him and paid for it, as well as Lanni's fudge-dipped cone, then casually continued the discussion. "Does the boy talk about his father much?"

"All the time. Some of the kids complain that Teddy's making it all up—that Mr. Mitchell couldn't possibly be as wonderful as Teddy says."

"And what do *you* think?"

Lanni pushed against the base of the counter with her sandaled foot, causing her stool to do a half turn so she faced Chandler. "I don't know Guy Mitchell. To my knowledge, he's never been to camp. One of his employees usually delivers and picks up Teddy." She frowned thoughtfully at the cone in her hand. "I think maybe Teddy has built up his father to be bigger than life in his own mind. I doubt if Mr. Mitchell is as perfect as Teddy says."

"Why do you think the boy would do that?"

What was he getting at? "I don't know. You tell me," she said bluntly. "You know him, don't you?"

"Guy Mitchell's been on the board at Scott-Hight for eight years or so. I've just known him a few months, and I know him in strictly a business sense, which doesn't put me in a position to comment on his family life."

"How often do you think an outsider can really tell what's going on in someone else's family?" she asked, thinking of the way her parents had maintained a public image of the perfect couple through forty years of ice-cold marriage. As far as they were concerned, appearances were everything. They hated each other, yet probably no one but Lanni and her brother were aware of that, thanks to the facade the Mercers presented to the rest of the world.

After a minute Lanni realized that Chandler hadn't answered her question. Glancing at him, she found him staring down at the countertop, his mouth etched with tight white lines. The stark loneliness in his expression dismayed her.

Her comment must have reminded him of whatever problems his own family had. Lanni cast about for something to say that would take away his unhappiness and when nothing came to mind, she spoke impulsively, without anticipating the consequences to herself. "Chandler, I've wanted to tell you...I'm really sorry about Scotty."

The lines around his mouth deepened and she heard his breath ease out in a quiet whoosh. When he looked up at her, his eyes seemed filled to the brim with something—something hard to define. It wasn't the hostility she'd suddenly been sure she would see there. It was a shimmering softness that might have been gratitude or simple sadness, edged with reserve.

"You knew Scotty?"

"I . . . no. I never met him." *Oh, please*, she thought frantically, *please don't drag the truth out of me.* But she couldn't lie to those searching, hurting dark eyes. She spoke in a near whisper. "You told me about him, a long time ago."

7

CHANDLER'S EXPRESSION changed fluidly, first startled, then considering, then puzzled. "You were serious. We really knew each other?" When she nodded, his look of perplexity deepened. "That's hard to believe."

Lanni carefully wrapped the remainder of her ice cream in a paper napkin and tossed in into a nearby trash receptacle. Her stomach leaden, she swiveled to face Chandler again. "Thanks very much."

He studied the delicate structure of her facial bones and the gold that highlighted her hair, thinking that this explained the nagging sense of familiarity about Lanni. "What I mean to say is, it's hard to believe I could have forgotten you."

"Why? I was just one of many girls for you."

Eyebrows lifting, he gave her a skeptical smile.

"Well, you *did* forget me," she pointed out calmly enough, controlling the urge to kick his shins.

He shook his head. "I couldn't have known you very well. Certainly not well enough to talk to you about my brother."

"You told me you thought he was dying."

Chandler gave another quick, negative head shake as he threw the rest of his cone in the trash. "That's impossible. I never talked about that. Just once . . ." He trailed off, frowning, then scrutinized her face with probing disbelief. "That was you? I knew you reminded me of someone, but your name didn't ring a bell."

"You called me Mercer," she said, her voice flat. "That year we thought it was cool to go by just our last names."

He stared at her intently, trying to remember that girl, Mercer. "Why didn't you tell me three days ago who you were?"

"You acted as if you'd never seen me before. I figured I couldn't have made a very lasting impression if you'd completely wiped the memory out of your mind."

With an almost imperceptible shudder, he looked away. "I did my best to wipe out that entire year."

"I wasn't as good as you are at forgetting," she muttered. She stood and walked out of the ice-cream shop, not caring if Chandler followed her. He did, slowly.

Once behind the wheel of the car, he turned to study the woman sitting beside him. He didn't bother telling her he'd never quite managed to forget the worst parts of that year. She would have no idea what he was talking about.

"You weren't exactly thrilled to see me again, were you?"

She glanced up at his sober question. He seemed sincerely puzzled. "Should I have been?" she wondered. "Most people wouldn't like to be reminded of the time they made a complete and utter fool of themselves." When he tilted his head and frowned at her, she explained with as much patience as she could muster.

"You were a first for me, Chandler. *The* first. But you . . . how many girls did you make love to that summer?" He looked blank, as she had expected. "You can't remember, can you? Probably two months after the fact, you couldn't have counted them, or recalled their faces, much less their names. But you see, *I* didn't sleep around. I thought sex was supposed to mean something. I thought I loved you. What's even funnier—" she gave a husky laugh that twisted like a knife in his stomach "—until you took off without a word, I honestly thought you cared, too."

Seeing from his expression that she was finally getting through to him, she went on bitterly. "I was a little slow about those things. It took me a week to realize you really weren't coming back to camp, that I'd just been a...a temporary convenience. I suppose I should have considered myself lucky that my first lover was the celebrated Chandler Scott."

Turning, he closed his hands over the steering wheel and stared at them in stunned silence. He looked as if she'd just hit him between the eyes with a brick.

"I hoped I'd never have to see you again," she said coolly. "I tried to forget. Dear Lord, I tried!" She gritted her teeth to stop herself from speaking aloud what she was thinking: *But every inch, every hair, every cell of your body was etched in my memory, and I couldn't get rid of it, no matter how hard I worked at it. I still can't.*

"Why are you telling me this?" His voice was hoarse.

She shrugged. "I don't know. I certainly didn't intend to. But I'm not sorry I did. And I *am* sorry about

Scotty." She clasped her hands together and discovered that her palms were moist and clammy. If she didn't get away from him soon, she thought she just might scream. "Now would you please take me back to camp?"

CHANDLER DIDN'T WANT to think about Lanni's revelation, but the knowledge that he'd hurt her badly kept intruding. He tried not to think at all—to just drive with his mind focused on the road—but a recurrent ache in his chest reminded him. No words came to him, or nothing that would help, at any rate, so in total silence he let Lanni out at the girls' dorm, then drove on to the administration building. Using the telephone there, he called the Muskegon airport and learned that he could get a late flight to Detroit with connections to Philadelphia. That would be simpler than rousing one of the company planes. Unable to find a note pad, he fished a Solo Enterprises deposit slip out of his wallet, scribbled a few hurried lines across the back of it and left it propped against the telephone.

Once he had packed and closed the cottage up, he drove out of camp without looking back. Lanni Mercer Preston followed him, though, every inch of the way to Muskegon, every blessed mile to Philadelphia. Her image filled his mind, while her soft, pained confession echoed in his head. "I'm sorry about Scotty...I tried to forget you...I thought you cared...I tried to forget..."

By the time he greeted Caroline at breakfast the next morning, his eyes were bleary and his nerves stretched taut from his efforts to shut Lanni out, to drive her back to the place where he locked up all his demons.

Caroline laid upon his forehead the same slim, tender hand that had searched for fever when he was small. "Are you ill, darling?"

"I'm okay. I came back early to review some figures for the board meeting Tuesday."

"You should have spent more time at Camp Ottawa, Chandler. I thought you were going to let George Wentworth handle that meeting."

"George isn't chairman of the board."

"But you said it wasn't an important meeting. You need more rest."

"I've been sleeping for three days." He hung on to his patience by reminding himself that she was just doing what she did best—being a mother. "Don't worry. I'll see that the meeting is short."

"And then you'll go back to Michigan?"

His abrupt and unequivocal refusal disturbed her. She didn't like the shadows that darkened his eyes. But they were familiar shadows. She'd seen them there often enough to realize she couldn't clear them away, no matter how much she would have liked to.

LANNI EXPECTED to hurt for a long time, to suffer serious regrets at having enlightened Chandler Scott about their shared history. A couple of days after he'd left camp, however, she made a startling discovery: she felt pretty darned good. A subtle metamorphosis had begun within her, sloughing off all her shame and bitterness, washing her clean from the inside out. Somehow, perhaps simply by confronting Chandler, she had nullified that mistake she'd made all those years ago. She had brought it out into the sunlight at long last, and now she could put it behind her.

It no longer seemed to matter that she'd once acted like a naive, impressionable fool. She'd made a life for herself in spite of the fact that Chandler had loved her and left her. Not a fascinating or wildly exciting life, but a good one. And Chandler had apparently been through his own trials. Being a Scott hadn't guaranteed that he would have unconditional happiness. The three days she had been around him had convinced her of that much.

Lanni spent a few more hours wondering exactly what experiences he'd undergone that had transformed him from a charming, if thoughtless, youth into the brooding man he was today. Maybe his brother's death had left Chandler feeling cheated, angry, rebellious. Maybe he'd just had to grow up before he was ready. Somehow she thought it was more complicated than that. She wished she could ask Don Grant what he knew of those missing years. Could Chandler have had a tragic love affair?

Disgusted at the romantic turn her imagination was taking, and at Don's failure to explain Chandler's most recent disappearance, Lanni vowed to concentrate on keeping the staff operating smoothly. On Sunday afternoon, kids and parents were already pouring into camp for the session that would start Monday. Since Don was busy manning the registration table in the eating lodge, up to his eyebrows in first-time campers and anxious mothers, Lanni decided it would be a good opportunity for her to clean the administration building. In all her last-minute preparations, she'd neglected Don's office, counting on his tidy habits to have kept the clutter to a minimum.

She had already swept and dusted the place and was emptying the small amount of trash from the wastebasket when her eye was caught by a fluttering, checkbook-sized piece of paper that bore Chandler's name. When she retrieved the paper from the top of the trash bag, she saw that it was an unused bank deposit slip for a company called Solo Enterprises, which had a Mesquite, Texas, address. The line below the company name read, Chandler Scott, President.

Curiosity gripped Lanni. So this was the development company, the one he'd built on his own. Solo Enterprises. It sounded…solitary. Strong. Successful. Not unlike Chandler himself.

Idly she turned the slip over and discovered a scrawled message on the back. "Don—I'm flying east tonight. You can catch me at Scott-Hight tomorrow if you think it's necessary, but you know better than to worry about what I'll report to the board. C.S."

Tracing the tip of one fingernail along the curve of his initials, she pictured Chandler's dark, restless form as he'd looked the last time she saw him, on the drive back from New Era. What had gone through his mind during that silent half hour in the car? Why had he decided to leave camp? Surely her revelation hadn't made him *that* uncomfortable!

But maybe it had. Chandler Scott had probably never been confronted by one of his victims before. Lanni Mercer at nineteen wouldn't have had the nerve to accuse a man of using her.

She chuckled, amused at the very idea that she should have been the one to send Chandler on a guilt trip, and pleased that she could laugh about it. It was good to know she was finally over the man.

Suddenly she stopped laughing and shivered instead, focusing on an intense mental image of Chandler. The man was 180 pounds of solid sex appeal. Mad, sad or indifferent, he could still drive her to distraction. She was only fooling herself if she thought for a minute that he didn't affect her. If he returned to camp today, she'd still be drawn to him by something she didn't understand.

Lanni stared at Chandler's note for another moment before, acting on a whim, she folded it and slid it into her pocket. A memento of her journey to womanhood, she told herself wryly.

"LANNI, ARE YOU SORRY you got a divorce?"

The question was unexpected, to say the least. For nearly an hour, Lanni had been engrossed in her sketching of the grassy dune where she sat, and in all that time Teddy Mitchell had lain on the sand a few feet away, as silent as she was. She'd actually forgotten he was there.

Shifting around on her three-legged stool, she glanced at the boy. Teddy had been in a strange, solitary mood lately.

"No," she said, "I can't say I've ever regretted my divorce. If anything, I wish I'd had the courage not to get married in the first place."

His brow furrowed. "You have something against marriage?"

"Actually I respect marriage. That's why I should never have married Tom. I knew very well I didn't love him."

"Then why'd you marry him?"

"Because my mother and father wanted me to."

The boy released his breath in a quick hiss of understanding. Lanni thought he'd probably spent most of his life trying to please his father or friends. She'd noticed often enough that he went to great lengths to win the approval of others.

"They made you marry a guy you didn't want to marry?"

"They didn't force me to, but their persuasive tactics were powerful. They managed to convince me I'd never amount to anything if I didn't go to the right university, associate with the right people, marry someone in the right social set. I guess maybe it took a thoroughly regrettable marriage to wise me up. All along I'd suspected Mother and Daddy were wrong, but after living for a year with the human iceberg my parents had picked out for me, I finally found the strength to assert my own wishes. Needless to say, the marriage didn't survive. My parents have little time for me these days. They consider me a failure."

Lanni's admission startled her almost as much as it must have shocked Teddy. She usually didn't talk about either her parents or her ex-husband. But she thought maybe it was time Teddy realized that a person couldn't always depend on his parents to supply his values—or his love. She was beginning to wonder if Mr. Mitchell gave Teddy the affection he so obviously craved.

As Teddy absorbed her words, Lanni turned back to her drawing pad and resumed sketching.

"You don't mind living alone?" he asked after a while, his voice low. "You don't get lonely?"

"Sure I do. But that's a poor reason to stay in a rotten marriage, or to get married in the first place. Married people can get lonely, too, you know."

He rolled onto his side, looking toward Lake Michigan. As she watched, he reached out and plucked a long blade of grass, then chewed on one end of it. "I never think of adults—*married* ones—as being lonely."

"I think," she said slowly, "the real answer is to be comfortable with yourself. To like yourself." Lanni didn't want to get a reputation among the kids as one who preached, but she hoped he understood what she meant. Heaven knew, the thing that had gotten her through the years since her divorce had been a satisfaction with her own company. Even so, her self-respect had sometimes taken a beating because of a few mistakes she'd made—mistakes like marrying Tom and sleeping with Chandler Scott.

Thank goodness she no longer felt compelled to berate herself for the past. The future . . .

"The future can hold whatever you want it to," she whispered.

"What?" Teddy sat up with a frown, and the stem of grass fell to the sand, forgotten.

"Nothing. Just talking to myself."

"Oh." Deciding the conversation was over, he got to his feet. "I guess I'll go see where everyone is."

Lanni fingered the grainy texture of her sketch pad. "Teddy, if you should ever want to talk about . . . well, about anything, I'll be glad to listen."

"I know." His eyes slid away from hers, then back. "Thanks, Lanni."

He retreated down the steep side of the dune before she had a chance to offer any more concrete help, and she had to content herself with the thought that the boy knew his friends at camp cared about him.

CHANDLER LET the Scott-Hight board meeting drag on longer than he intended, primarily because his mind wasn't entirely on the subject. Toward the end, his brief informal report on Camp Ottawa triggered a discussion among the rest of the board members about the possibility of increasing the number of subsidies awarded each year to needy youngsters. Although almost everyone liked the idea, a couple of hold-outs felt they should look into the matter further, perhaps by means of a committee to study the question.

Chandler considered that a stalling tactic to kill the issue. "No committee," he said. "I've never yet seen a committee that could agree on anything."

"But we need more specific information before we vote. We need figures on how many of our scholarship recipients are now tax-paying members of society. . ."

Although he struggled to concentrate, Chandler kept losing his focus, envisioning the tall, slender woman with tousled chestnut hair and soft gray eyes full of reproach for the selfish, thoughtless youth he'd been at twenty-one. As he replayed faint memories of that long-ago evening on the sand dunes and his hasty departure later that night, a shell of despair grew around his heart. He'd had a reason for never wanting to remember anything about that year. But Lanni didn't know that, and he wasn't about to enlighten her. She would just have to keep on hating him.

Brushing a hand across his eyes in frustration, he interrupted the long-winded old skinflint who believed charity should begin, and most certainly end, at home. "It sounds to me, Leonard, as if you're out of touch with the camping programs." *If you were ever in touch,* he tacked on silently. "I'd like you to spend a couple of days at Camp Ottawa. I want you to take a close look at things and judge for yourself if we're throwing away our money." He turned to a handsome, suntanned blond man seated nearby. "Guy, why don't you go along with Leonard. Keep him company, make sure he gets a well-rounded view of things."

Teddy Mitchell's father glanced up in surprise. "You want me to visit camp?"

Chandler nodded. "You two can report back to the rest of us a week from today."

"But I can't make it before then, Chandler. My horse farm—"

"Your horses can wait," Chandler said, his smile pleasant, his tone firm. It was his best chairman-of-the-board voice, designed to disarm his opponent subtly, like a velvet-sheathed sword. Guy Mitchell wore a look of poorly concealed vexation the rest of the meeting, but Chandler ignored it. Let the man spend a little time with his son, he thought. Even if Guy didn't do it voluntarily, perhaps it would help the boy.

And what will help you, he asked himself as he returned to his office after adjourning the meeting. A dozen mea culpas? Maybe a brand spanking new lady with no memories attached?

He slapped his briefcase down on top of his desk and began sorting through the papers inside. Without pausing, he called in his secretary and told her to arrange for one of the company jets to be ready in an hour and a half to fly him to Dallas. Maybe that was what he needed.

8

LANNI CHECKED her daily list of things to be done three times before she felt sure she hadn't overlooked anything. It was the second Friday of the first camp session, and things were running too smoothly for her peace of mind. She kept expecting a disaster to hit, most likely just when she was relaxing on the beach, lulled half to sleep by the sun. Either a washing machine would go berserk and flood the linen room with sudsy water, or someone would leave the freezer door ajar, causing a month's supply of hamburger meat to thaw.

In truth, she figured neither of these dire events was going to transpire, but rather than risk it, she pushed herself much harder than she did the staff. It had been days since she'd even thought of sketching or sunbathing. She double-checked the various crews so often that the kids thought she'd lost confidence in them.

She hadn't. She just felt driven, too charged with energy to sit still. Her restlessness had a source—a face and voice that kept cropping up whenever things got quiet. And those dark, smoldering eyes that haunted her had a way of melting every rational bone in her body and causing her to daydream about what would happen if Chandler Scott returned to Camp Ottawa.

Fantasies like that, she didn't need. Good grief, she knew better. She was smart now, mature. She knew she could handle a relationship with him, just the way she'd come out of their most recent encounter in better shape emotionally than she'd ever been before. She knew what she could do, so she didn't need to prove anything.

Besides, she should be directing all this excess energy toward helping Teddy Mitchell. The thing was, she had no idea what was going on in his head. She had thought his father's visit last week would have cheered up the boy, but Teddy's mask was more firmly in place than ever. None of Lanni's concerned overtures got past the wall of his smile.

Tossing down her ball-point pen in frustration, Lanni glanced around the linen room. The grounds crew were out in the woods in the open-air amphitheater, preparing the pit for the ceremonial council fire that the campers would attend that evening. The linen staff were on their regular rounds of scrubbing toilets and showers in the remote bathhouses. The kitchen workers would start supper in another hour. There was no reason for Lanni to hang around waiting for something to go wrong. She would take some time off and go for a long walk.

Ten minutes later she was striding along the hiking trail toward the Scott cottage, telling herself that she did need the exercise and that it wouldn't be a bad idea to make sure the house was locked up. It hadn't been occupied since Chandler had left camp two weeks ago.

When the cushion of fallen leaves beneath her feet ended and Lanni emerged from the woods, she came to a precipitous halt, her pulse stuttering wildly. A white Pontiac parked under the porte cochere, its trunk open, gave her the unsettling impression that the place was in use, after all. Or in the process of being burglarized.

Lanni swallowed what felt like her heart and ordered her legs to move forward again. Could this just be a hallucination? Don would surely have told her if they were expecting visitors. The car looked like another rental job. Since thieves usually stole automobiles rather than renting them, she hoped she could rule out the burglary possibility.

Of course, it could be Chandler.

Lanni glanced around suspiciously. Where had that suggestion come from? Did she want it to be Chandler?

She was close enough by now to reach out and touch the car, and when her fingertips met the hot polished surface of a rear fender, she acknowledged that this was no figment. This was the fruit of Detroit. Its trunk was carpeted, clean as a pin and empty. If someone was robbing the place, Lanni still had time to call the sheriff. If it was a dignitary paying a visit, however, she was too late; he'd already moved in, lock, stock and barrel.

When the cottage's screen door swung open and the "dignitary" stepped outside wearing nothing but his sexy white swimsuit, Lanni guessed that her most dangerous fantasies were about to be put to the test. Chandler Scott had indeed returned to Camp Ottawa. Every gorgeous, dark-skinned inch of him.

CHANDLER HADN'T BEEN ABLE to find the paperback mystery novel he'd picked up at the airport gift shop. Thinking he must have dropped it while unloading the car, he was retracing his steps when he saw that he'd left the trunk lid wide open. Where was his mind these days?

And then he saw Lanni Preston leaning against the fender as if she needed the support, and he felt as shattered as she looked.

Not yet, he thought. He wasn't supposed to run into her yet. He hadn't psyched himself up to withstand her anger. He'd done well just to convince himself he had a perfect right to be here.

Anyway, she was the cause of his absent-mindedness. She'd rendered him about as useful as a computer without a program. He couldn't keep his mind on anything anymore, and he intended to do something about it. But he wasn't quite ready.

Lanni waited a moment for her heartbeat to slow down, or for Chandler to say something, and when neither of those happened, she managed a rather breathless greeting. "Hello, Chandler."

He moved just enough to let the door thud shut behind him, watching her like a hawk. She was even lovelier than he'd remembered. She had on a pink-and-white wide-striped shirt, jeans and white huaraches, and her hair was long and loose and clean. A sudden familiar urge gripped him to capture a handful of that chestnut silk and rub it across his skin, to savor its texture. Only the tight clenching of his fist stopped him from acting on that impulse. "Hello, Lanni."

Hearing the wariness in his voice, she relaxed. The man was obviously terrified of a scene. His muscles were flexed, tensed as if for battle.

"This is a surprise," she said. "Don didn't tell me you were planning to come back."

Her smooth tone, devoid of bitterness, gave him pause. Wasn't she mad at him? "Don didn't know," he said cautiously. "I decided to come on the spur of the moment, so I didn't have time to call ahead." He seemed to hesitate, then drew a quick breath. "I'm sorry you had no warning."

For some crazy reason Lanni felt on top of the world, with energy buzzing in her veins, revving her up like a teenager. She made a dismissive gesture with one hand. "No problem. The linen crew cleaned your place thoroughly last week, but I'll check right now to see if it needs to be gone over again."

"That's not necessary. The place looks fine."

"Have you looked under the beds lately?" she asked with a grin. "I can clean out the dust bunnies at least."

"Please don't bother." He sounded a bit strained. "I was planning to be out myself."

Lanni noted the large brown towel slung over one broad shoulder and the sun shades dangling from his right hand. "You're going down to the beach, hmm? Well, go ahead. I wouldn't want to disturb you."

Was she being sarcastic? He couldn't tell. For the first time in his life, Chandler didn't know how to treat a woman. It was a most uncomfortable feeling.

She took a couple of steps toward the door, intending to enter the house and get to work, but Chandler continued to stand there with that slight frown on his face, blocking her way. "Excuse me," she finally said, and the dry amusement in her voice nudged him into action.

He moved to one side without speaking and opened the screen door for her. As soon as she had disappeared into the house, he let the door shut by itself, slammed the car trunk and then headed straight for the beach as if he'd had a narrow escape.

She took the broom out of the closet and put it to use, thinking that being face-to-face with Chandler Scott had proved she was over her feelings of having been victimized.

On the other hand, it had also proved she wasn't over the attraction to Chandler, so maybe his getaway had been closer than he knew. She'd never met a man who appealed more to her physical senses. She liked the way he looked and smelled and felt, and now that her reason wasn't clouded by an old anger, she acknowledged that he could be interesting and fun to be around. He was, after all, witty and intelligent and charismatic. And she wasn't sure if that was good or not.

At any rate, it was definitely distracting. She had absolutely no interest in getting her work done, other than as an excuse to spy on Chandler.

He had, she soon discovered, chosen the same corner bedroom that he'd used on his last visit. His tan leather suitcase lay open on the bed, and it was full of clothes. Which could mean, she told herself with an unconscious smile, that he planned to stay awhile.

She hurried back downstairs to check out the refrigerator and found it empty except for a bag of fruit and a gallon of milk. Her smile faded. Even taking into account the canned goods in the cabinet, a man couldn't subsist for very long on just milk and grapes.

She gave the refrigerator door a disgruntled shove to close it, muttering, "Shoot!"

"Is something wrong?"

Whirling, she discovered Chandler watching her from the doorway, his expression guarded.

What was he doing back already? He'd barely been gone ten minutes. How embarrassing to get caught snooping!

"I just noticed that your refrigerator is almost empty," she said sheepishly.

Nodding, he draped the towel over the back of the kitchen chair and laid his sunglasses on the counter. "I thought I'd eat at the dining hall." Dark, unreadable eyes swung on her. "If that's okay."

Relief made her flippant. "Why not? It's your money."

The instant she spoke, she would have given anything to take back the words. It was his money, all right, but that had nothing to do with anything. Even if it hadn't been his family that funded the camp and paid her salary every summer, Lanni would have wanted him there, across the table from her three times a day.

While she was still searching for a way to erase her answer, she saw his chin jut out and his eyes flare with very understandable annoyance. She expected a snappy comeback, but instead he nodded again, turned on his heel and left the room.

Wincing, she listened to the muffled sound of his bare feet ascending the stairs. *Way to go, Lanni*, she congratulated herself, as she got down to business sweeping the kitchen and living room. She could probably write a book on how to make a lousy impression on men.

Just as she stood debating the wisdom of trying to sweep the upper floor with an irate Chandler in residence, he came back down the stairs, fully dressed in jeans and a soft white shirt and Topsiders.

He paused on the bottom step, one hand on the newel post, and took a slow, steadying breath. *Now*, he thought. "I'd like to have a word with you, please."

Lanni had backed up against the wall and was holding on to the broom handle for security. At his quiet request—or was it an order?—she felt her stomach turn upside down.

She gave him a weak smile. "Of course."

They sat down in the living room on sofas that faced each other. Like two adversaries, it seemed to Chandler. Only so far she hadn't acted the way he'd figured she would. She'd just made that one crack about his money, and he'd seen that she regretted it right away. But the anger had to be there still, somewhere, perhaps deep inside her. After all, she'd spend a lot of years hating him.

He opened his mouth to speak and closed it again, his eyes edging away from hers. What could he say? Had he really believed he was prepared for this? Gritting his teeth, he forced himself to meet her gray gaze. "I don't know how to go about this," he said in a low voice. "I'm not very good at making apologies."

He wanted to apologize? A taut spring in Lanni's chest popped loose. She could handle this.

"You're not good at it? I never would have guessed."

Her humorous tone took him aback. Leaning against the sofa cushions, he studied her searchingly for a moment. "I had a hard enough time apologizing for my rudeness the last time I was here. What can I say now? I'm sorry I gave you cause to hate men?"

"But I don't hate men."

"Just me, hmm?"

"Not even you."

He considered that before deciding that it didn't really matter whether she knew she hated him. The fact was, she had every right to be mad as hell at being seduced and then forgotten. Come to think of it, he'd done that to a lot of women in his time. There was no excusing it, not even taking into account his reasons for wanting to forget that year in particular—the awful truth he'd discovered after Scotty died. Up until then, he'd been totally spoiled and self-indulgent. The only other human beings he'd ever loved more than himself had been his family; afterward, he'd had to handle losing not just Scotty but his parents, too, and the only life he'd ever known. He guessed he hadn't done a very good job of handling things.

He said tightly, "I'm sorry I hurt you, Lanni."

He might have thought of something more to say, but she interrupted him calmly. "Apology accepted."

His mouth snapped shut and he frowned at her. "Just like that?"

"Yes."

He stood up and walked around the room, then stopped in front of her with his hands in his pockets. "Don't you think it's ten years too late?"

Once, not very long ago, she would have agreed with him. Now it seemed she had to persuade him his apology was worth something. What a turnaround!

"Too late for what? To change what happened? Nobody can do that. But I don't believe it's ever too late to apologize." She stood, too, which put her within range of his captivating male fragrance and made her breath catch with pleasure. Heart pounding, she gazed into his black velvet eyes and felt the tingling response tighten her breasts, then slowly radiate through her abdomen to her pelvis and all the way down to her toes. She extended her hand. "Pax?"

He seemed to be boring a hole in her, he was staring so intently. Finally he inclined his dark head and translated the Latin for *peace* into Spanish. "*Paz.*"

Against his better judgment, he took the hand she offered him. His big brown hand enveloped hers in a warm clasp, and he didn't want to let go. The touch of her smooth palm against his subtly ensnared him. Signals of need shot out from their joined fingers, skimming along the nerves in his arm and from there to every vital part of his body. He felt his blood quicken and a sweet ache of longing settle between his thighs. His eyes glittered with the potency of the connection between them.

She could barely breathe. Just when she thought she would be consumed from within by the pulsating heat in her bloodstream, Chandler dropped her hand and pulled his own back, shoving it in his pocket. He had the look of a man who didn't know exactly what hit him. She wondered whether he found the supercharged atmosphere as bewitching as she did. The electricity in the air between them seemed so much more compelling than it had been ten years ago. It made her feel weak and yet fully, gloriously alert. It made her feel wonderful!

"If you really want peace," she suggested solemnly, forcing herself to suppress her body's responses to him, "you'll put your experience where your mouth is." His dark, arching brows lifted in question. "I'm talking about your renowned housekeeping talents." She stuck out the broom to him. "You sweep upstairs. I'll dust."

Her eyes were shaded the same pearl gray of a dove in flight across a clear sky. As hard as he looked, he saw no accusation in their depths. He did see a flicker of something, however, that matched what he'd been experiencing for the past ten minutes. He dragged his hand out of his pocket and accepted the wooden handle of the broom without a word.

Working in total silence, they finished cleaning up the cottage in thirteen minutes flat by the clock over the living room mantel. Lanni couldn't help marveling at Chandler's willingness to lend a hand, not to mention his unexpected apology. It was obvious that he hadn't just laughed off her revelation about their previous relationship, nor could he quite bring himself to trust her forgiveness, because he didn't realize how sick and tired she was of holding a grudge. She was eager to forget, while he—he'd just recently faced the knowledge of the effect he'd had on her. Oddly, he'd taken it to heart far more than she'd ever anticipated he would.

Lanni sighed at the complexity of the situation. It was disconcerting to have to revise her opinion of Chandler Scott after having him head her list of ten most wanted criminals for so long. Strange to discover that he had a conscience.

Was he busy reassessing her, too? Was that why, whenever she looked up from dusting the furniture, she found him watching her obliquely, his face unreadable? Or was his awareness of her simply another result of the distinct sexual tension that permeated whatever room they shared?

Perhaps it was a little of both. At any rate, when Chandler had returned the broom and dust rag to the storage closet downstairs, and Lanni had made a mental note of how many sheets and towels should be brought over from the linen room, he leaned against the doorjamb and regarded her openly.

Nervous at the prolonged silence, Lanni said brightly, "I think I'll just run over and get the towels and things you'll need while you're here."

And when she would have gone, he reached out and caught her arm to stop her. "Lanni, there's something I want to tell you about that time we knew each other."

"You don't have to tell me anything," she said softly.

"I want you to understand," he said, although the Lord knew he didn't want to talk about this. "The reason I left camp so suddenly. . . the only reason I didn't at least say goodbye was that I got a message in the middle of the night from my father, asking me to return to Philadelphia at once." He looked past her shoulder, out the windows. Along the horizon, a thin strip of Lake Michigan shone white in the afternoon sun. "My brother was dying. I had been right about that."

Unmindful of the fierce grip of his fingers on her arm, she shook her head slowly. "I didn't know—"

His curt nod stopped her. "He lived two more weeks after I got there, but he was unconscious the whole time."

When he paused, she spoke uncertainly. "I remember that you mentioned the possibility of a kidney transplant for Scotty." Actually what Chandler had told her was that he hoped to qualify as a kidney donor for his brother.

"It was never an option." His bleak eyes stared beyond Lanni, and she guessed that he was seeing another time, another place entirely. He released her arm and raked his fingers through his hair, his mouth compressed. "Scotty was in no shape to undergo surgery. By the time I got there, he was suffering from congestive heart failure. Finally his heart gave out completely." He averted his head. "I never got a chance to tell him goodbye."

Lanni's eyes burned with unshed tears. Was it any wonder he'd pushed that summer out of his mind?

With considerable effort, he focused on her again, his features taut. "I was twenty-one years old, a kid. I was selfish and spoiled and just about any other unpleasant adjective you want to call me. I wasn't ready to marry anyone. But I should have told you I was leaving." His hand made a small gesture toward her, then fell to his side. "I wanted you to know the reason I didn't."

His earlier apology had already earned her forgiveness. Now her soft heart went out to him. "Thank you for telling me," she whispered, reaching for his hand.

When his fingers instinctively entwined with hers, she guessed that he was being driven by a deep, aching loneliness. Whether he was responsible for creating his own solitary existence, she didn't know. At the moment, it didn't really matter.

Lanni took one more step forward and pulled her hand free in order to slide her arms around his waist. She gave him a tight squeeze that was part comfort, part pure enjoyment of his hard, distinctly masculine physique. After a fractional hesitation, he gave in and hugged her back.

She felt like heaven to him. Even so, Chandler didn't let himself hold her the way he wanted. It would be so easy to get lost in her sweetness, in her consoling arms. But he refused to get caught up in the gentle compassion that was pushing her now. In fact, he wasn't looking for a relationship of any kind. There were too many ugly secrets in his past.

9

FEELING HIS NEED GROW with every second that he pressed her close, Chandler slowly, reluctantly disengaged himself from her embrace and gave Lanni a crooked smile. "Would it surprise you to know I'm hungry?"

She was hungry, too, but not for anything as ordinary as food. Already missing his warm arms, she concentrated on the incredible whiteness of his smile. "You wouldn't be male if you weren't hungry. Can you wait until supper?"

He checked his watch. "A whole hour?" He sounded doubtful. "I don't know. I didn't get to eat lunch."

Grinning, she punched his shoulder with a slender fist. "Buck up, old boy. I'll put you to work setting tables in the eating lodge and maybe we'll get to eat early."

Her teasing relieved Chandler's tension. "First you make me sweep my own house," he grumbled as they went out to the car and started back to headquarters. "Now you want me to work in the kitchen. You don't seem to have much respect for the chairman of the board at Scott-Hight, Ms Preston."

"That's because I've never seen you chairman-of-the-board types do much except laze around in the sun and eat huge quantities of camp cuisine. I figure that with the proper encouragement, you and all the rest of your lofty board can become productive members of society."

"And you plan to provide the encouragement?"

"Just doing my civic duty."

"Gee, thanks," he said dryly.

"I'm always glad to help."

He eased the car past some of the grounds crew who were walking in the same direction along the paved road, and Lanni waved at the boys.

"Did you have any success reforming Leonard Wilson and Guy Mitchell when they were here last week?" Chandler asked.

"Are you kidding? *You* may wield a mean mop, but those guys are hopeless! They must have full-time maids to follow them around at home, picking up after them. In the two days they spent at camp, I had to send the linen crew over twice to clean up, because they kept complaining the place was messy. It was messy, all right, and I can tell you exactly how it got that way."

He threw back his dark head and laughed, delighted at Lanni in this irreverent mood.

"By the way, Mr. Chairman, are you the one who's responsible for their visit?" she demanded. When he acknowledged that he was, she shook her head, no longer joking. "I see now why Teddy has problems."

"Why?"

"His father is supercritical of him. You wouldn't believe how hard Ted tried to please him, but he couldn't seem to do enough. Mr. Mitchell kept finding fault, picking away at every little thing from his table man-ners to the clothes he wore. He acted as if he blamed Teddy for his having to be here when he'd rather have been home with his horses."

As he parked by the loading dock, Chandler muttered a quiet "Hmph!" Mitchell's report to the board had omitted any such unpleasantness. As a matter of fact, he'd been instrumental in helping convince Leonard Wilson that establishing more subsidies was a reasonable goal.

From Chandler's expression of disappointment, Lanni figured that he'd set up Guy Mitchell's visit primarily to benefit Teddy, and her estimation of his character shot up several more notches. He wasn't nearly as wrapped up in himself as she had once thought.

Don't get carried away, she cautioned herself. The man was only human. Actually, it was that imperfect quality about him that appealed to her the most, she thought.

Anyway, it was *one* of his most appealing qualities. During supper she noticed a lot of his others. So did the female staff members at the table, none of whom cared that he belonged to that ignominious category of the over-thirty.

"Why don't you come to the council fire, Mr. Scott?" Penny asked.

"Is that tonight?"

"Uh-huh. The kids—" the way she said it, Penny might have been long-past her teen years "—have been bragging all week about how neat the program's going to be."

He looked thoughtful. "The campers run the show, hmm? It's been a while since I had a chance to watch the ceremonies, but I used to enjoy them."

"They're terrific," Don Grant said. "You really should come, Chandler."

Chandler's glance flicked toward Lanni and connected with hers for an electric moment, shocking her to the center of her being before he dragged his eyes away and smiled at his eager feminine audience. "Maybe so. We'll have to see if it can be arranged."

Which left Lanni wondering just what there was to arrange. Either he wanted to attend, or he didn't.

Unless... perhaps he had in mind arranging to accompany the rest of that "we" in his "we'll have to see." And who might that "we" be? Lanni?

She sat up straighter and tried to will her cheeks not to radiate such heat. Good grief, she was blushing! She was supposed to be more mature than those giggling teenagers across the table.

Supper finished, Lanni had just ordered herself to stop dreaming up feeble excuses to linger when she spotted a twelve-year-old beanpole with jet black hair and brown skin zeroing in on the table, shouting, "¡Amigo! ¡Buenas dias!"

Chandler got to his feet just in time to catch the youngster as he leaped for a bear hug. "Hey, *compadre. ¿Que pasa?*"

Lanni understood that much of the exchange, but at that point her meager command of the Spanish language failed her. The two friends began firing questions and answers back and forth at each other in what sounded like a confusing tangle of English and Spanish. Both seemed so oblivious of anyone else in the busy lodge that Lanni and Don sat back and grinned at each other as they eavesdropped.

She heard the camper say, "I *knew* you'd come to see me," and "You were right. I love Michigan," but the rest was beyond her.

As for Chandler, he lapsed into his Harvard English from time to time as he searched for an elusive phrase, and Lanni imagined that she could tell a big difference between his accent and the child's, but still he was no slouch in the Spanish department. And the kid obviously adored him. From a word snatched here and there, she gathered that the boy was responding to Chandler's enquiries about his swimming and sailing experiences at Camp Ottawa, and about his family down in the Rio Grande Valley.

A few minutes later, as Lanni watched Chandler and his youthful amigo stroll out the door together, the boy still talking ninety miles a minute while the man listened, she felt her smile lose some of its gusto. There went her big hopes for the evening.

"Cute kid," she said when she saw Don regarding her knowingly. "Those two seem to have a language of their own."

Don nodded. "Tex-Mex."

"Pardon?"

"That's what they call it in Texas, where Chandler picked it up. It's a corruption of formal Spanish. You won't find it in any textbook."

She tilted her head in thought. "Chandler surprises me. I would have figured him for a Latin or Greek scholar, considering his Ivy League background."

"He certainly is a master of the unexpected, all right. It's as though he's a different person from the Chandler I used to know."

Could Don actually be presenting her with an opening to talk about the boss? If so, Lanni didn't want to blow it. "I've noticed," she said.

The business manager gave a slow nod. "I'd forgotten you two were friends."

"For a short while, a very long time ago."

"Well, anyway, you know what I mean about the changes in his personality. You must have known how close he was to his brother, so the kidney disease research center that he established probably doesn't surprise you."

Even as she was thinking, *What kidney disease research center?* Don went on.

"But the young Chandler was a bit of a snob, even if he was basically a good kid. I can't see him taking an interest in a boy like Pete Escabedo there. Chandler had never even met a migrant worker, which is what Pete's parents were before Chandler sponsored them in job training. Besides that, he's provided the family with food and clothes and is sending Pete to camp and his sister to college." Don saw the expression on Lanni's face. "By the way, Chandler didn't tell me any of this. Pete did. And I feel sure Chandler would rather not have that information broadcast around, for a lot of reasons. You'll keep his secret, won't you?"

That he wasn't the hardened cynic he sometimes seemed to be? Yes, Lanni wouldn't advertise the fact. But she couldn't exactly forget it, either. It was just one more confusing aspect of his considerable mystique that she had to get used to.

As she sat at dusk with several of her staff on the uppermost tier of Camp Ottawa's large stone council circle, she saw Chandler and Pete Escabedo enter across the way. Pete thumped his friend on the arm in silent goodbye and went to sit with his cabin mates, leaving Chandler standing with his hands in his pockets, glancing around the amphitheater.

Even though Lanni pretended an interest in the goings-on down in the fire pit, she knew the moment Chandler picked her out of the crowd. A glowing warmth suffused her, bringing instant relief from the chill of twilight in the Michigan woods. She felt compelled to look back at him, and when she did she realized he seemed completely, starkly alone. His dark eyes watched her, waiting, but for what?

Acting on an unconscious order from her heart, she waved at him, inviting him over.

Then, before he could respond, Lanni jerked her hand down and turned away. *Idiot*, she thought. Chandler didn't need anyone to feel sorry for him for his solitude. He could snap his fingers and have every female in sight jumping to eager attention.

A minute later, feeling a firmly muscled body squeeze down into the limited space beside her, she lifted her lashes and stared at Chandler.

Seeing her surprise, he stopped trying to wedge himself in between her and Denise. "I thought you were waving at me."

The tightness in her chest suddenly loosened, and she scooted over against Jack Mills to give Chandler another couple of inches. "I was. Is that better?"

He relaxed, too. "A little. Now I can breathe, at least."

Lanni should have been able to breathe better than she was doing. But it was hard to get her body coordinated when she was squashed right up against Chandler. All along her right side, she felt the heat and shape of his shoulder, hip and thigh. Every time he shifted a bit, getting comfortable on the unyielding seat, some new, interesting part of him touched her, and a charge of high-voltage awareness jagged through her like a bolt of lightning. Her heart was racing and her pulse had gone completely haywire, and the sexy male scent that clung to him only added to her respiratory distress.

Chandler probably thought she had some kind of nervous disorder, she decided when his shoulder rubbed against hers in a disturbingly familiar way and she almost jumped a foot.

She spoke up hurriedly. "I hope they light the council fire soon. It's getting so dark, I can't see a thing."

"This isn't bad." His head was bent, his voice husky and very low, so she alone could hear him. Despite the noisy chatter that surrounded them, there was an intimacy to the moment that enthralled her. "I've always liked these woods at night. Look up at the trees." Obeying him, she focused on the black feathery bottoms of the branches splayed overhead against a sky streaked by mauve and vermilion. "Nice, hmm? Feel that shiver run down your spine?"

She felt a shiver, all right. She just wasn't entirely certain it could be attributed to the beauty of the night.

Swallowing hard, she nodded and felt his mouth brush her temple. The caressing touch of his lips on her skin caused her shiver to become externalized, so that Chandler felt her trembling.

"Are you cold?" he asked. "You should have worn a sweater."

"I forgot to p-put it on my list."

Her teeth chattered so noisily that Chandler had no choice but to wrap his left arm around her and try to infuse her with his warmth. He suddenly had plenty to spare. Something had just kindled a raging fire in the pit of his stomach, and the flames were infiltrating his blood, sneaking along forbidden pathways.

Lord, what was he doing? He'd ordered himself not to even think about touching her, because he'd suspected he could never again be casual where Lanni was concerned. He should turn her loose right now and let her warm herself. Instead, he threw caution to the wind. Sliding his hand beneath the ribbed cotton of her pullover top, he drew her closer and savored the pliant way she molded to fit against his side.

With the crown of her head resting beneath his jaw, his palm curved warm and rough against the satin skin of her waist, she soon grew drunk on the feel of Chandler. "Mmm...nice!" she whispered lightly. He had her sweater beat by a mile! "Do you suppose I could hire you for the winter?"

"Maybe. Make me an offer."

"In what price range? I'm not sure I can afford you."

He gave a soft, devilish laugh, then fell abruptly silent as a dark form stepped to the center of the arena floor below and struck a spark to the waiting pyramid of tree limbs. A moment later the bonfire was fully ablaze, casting a red-orange glow on the council circle.

Mindful of the flickering light and the kids around them, Chandler pulled his hand out from under her shirt and laid it on her silky thigh, then gulped and transferred it to his own lap. Nothing was safe at this point.

He tried very hard to ignore Lanni and pay attention, as a youth in deerskin pants and moccasins addressed the crowd. "Welcome to the council fire, fellow braves and visitors. Tonight the warriors in cabins six and seven will present the story of Michigan, home of the great Ottawa nation."

There followed the most unusual depiction of history that either Lanni or Chandler had ever seen, beginning with a group of native Americans sitting around the campfire smoking long pipes. The Indians were discussing what to name their village.

Making much of the fact that their cluster of wigwams rose out of a swampy area, where their moccasins were forever bogging down in mud, they heeded the suggestion of a disgruntled squaw to call the place *Mash-Kig-Gong*, meaning *river with marshes*. From that, the narrator explained in an aside, the white set-

tlement later built at the same location became Muskegon.

Subsequent scenes showed the Frenchman Adrien
Jolliet exploring Michigan and sending back to Que-
bec enthusiastic reports about the possibilities for fur
trappers in the lower peninsula. "You wouldn't believe
all the foxes I've seen!" the squeaky-voiced Jolliet told
his messenger. He used both hands to trace an hour-
glass shape while keeping his eyes on a nearby Indian
maiden whose figure had been improved with plenty
of tissue-paper stuffing. The audience laughed, as intended.

Skipping over years and details, the players acted out
sketches of Michigan's admission to the Union in 1837
as the twenty-sixth state, its development as the leading lumber-producing state, and then the building of the
first automobile factory in Lansing in 1897, one year
after Henry Ford completed his first gasoline-driven
car.

According to the preteen authors of this pageant, the
final significant event in Michigan's history took place
in 1920 and concerned a very rich, very exasperated
gentleman named Grosvenor Scott, far away in Penn-
sylvania.

"Picture a mansion that makes the White House look
like a shanty," the narrator instructed them.

Just then a rather husky adolescent wearing one of
Don Grant's suit coats entered with his wife, whose sole
claim to femininity was the long stringy "hair" that had
once graced a mop in the linen room.

"My dear," Grosvenor Scott said in a pseudo-upper-class British accent, "that boy of yours has me at my wit's end. Why, do you know what he did today? He locked the chauffeur in the butler's pantry with the maid!"

"Oh, dear me!" Mrs. Scott answered in a quavering falsetto. "*Your* son is a regular hooligan."

"A what?"

"A juvenile delinquent."

"Oh, yes. Quite right."

Despite the amused titters from the rest of the audience, Lanni noticed to her discomfort that Chandler was silent. She could have predicted that he wouldn't consider his family history anything to joke about. Oh, Lord! Heads would probably roll when this was over.

Onstage, the actors were unaware of a problem. After some discussion, the Scotts decided that the boy Winston simply had an excess of energy and needed a chance to experience life to the fullest, under competent supervision, preferably in an outdoor setting. Preferably far enough away from Philadelphia that they would be cushioned from the effects of his mischief. And surely, the parents concluded, there must be other youngsters—not to mention parents—who could benefit from the same sort of vigorous activity program that they had in mind for Winston.

"I have it! We'll found a summer camp!" Mr. Scott said, pounding Mrs. Scott on the back with such enthusiasm that Mrs. Scott's makeshift wig flew off.

Everyone in the audience roared. When Lanni heard Chandler's quiet chuckle, she felt a surge of relief.

In the midst of the laughter, Mrs. Scott retrieved the mop head and slapped it back in place. "Well done, Grovy! Let's build this camp somewhere in the heart of America. May I suggest Michigan! And let's call it something Indian, shall we?"

"How does 'Camp Ottawa' strike you?"

"I love it! Where is that boy of yours? We simply must tell him our news. Winston! Oh, Winston!"

"WELL? Is that how the idea for Camp Ottawa really came about?" Lanni asked as they strolled back along the road toward headquarters. The crisscrossing beams of a hundred flashlights arced through the darkness around them.

Chandler's arm brushed Lanni's from time to time, but otherwise he didn't touch her. She knew she was crazy to wish he would try to warm her up again. Surrounded by campers and staff, the night woods echoing with noisy horseplay, he could hardly be blamed for not feeling amorous.

"I don't know," Chandler said. "I wasn't around in 1920." He resolutely kept his hands to himself and refused to speculate whether Lanni might still be cold.

"But surely you know the real poop. I'll bet the true version is inscribed in your family Bible, right there in black and white, so you can pass it down to all the little future Scotts."

He jammed his hands in his pockets. This wasn't the time or place to tell her that if the world was waiting for him to carry on the noble Scott name, it would have a long wait indeed.

"I imagine what we saw tonight was close enough to the truth," he said after an uncomfortable pause.

With a silent sigh, Lanni apologized softly. "I'm sorry I keep bringing up something you don't like to talk about."

"Forget it."

"Okay, but I hope the play didn't offend you. The kids meant no harm—"

"For pete's sake, Lanni," he interrupted swiftly, his voice tight, "I wasn't offended. Why should I be? From all accounts, Winston Scott was something of a hooligan, all right, even in his later years. Listen." He drew her out of the stream of traffic that dwindled as campers and counselors veered off on footpaths to their cabins deeper in the woods. Only the service staff remained in a pack on the main road, and they quickly left Lanni and Chandler behind. "You quit apologizing to me, and I won't apologize to you anymore. There is such a thing as too much humility."

She stood close to him, barely able to concentrate on his words while his fingers clasped her wrist so firmly. It was as if they were both magnetized, fused together with a galvanic energy. "We...we have been doing quite a bit of that today, haven't we?"

He nodded and reached for her other arm. *Don't*, he warned himself and then promptly ignored the warning. Pulling her against him, he slid both arms around behind her back and pressed her to his length. His fingers wove into the heavy silky mass of her hair and he inhaled deeply, drawing her fragrance into his lungs. When his brain registered the slender, supple feel of her body within his arms, her smooth cheek against his throat, a moan started deep in his chest, and with gut-wrenching effort he managed to keep it down there.

"Lanni, I want to see you tomorrow night," he said hoarsely.

She wanted to stay right there, plastered tight against him, until tomorrow night, or until he did something to satisfy the awesome hunger that gnawed at her. She nuzzled his throat and hugged him back to see if that helped, but it didn't. It only made the hunger sharper. It also seemed to be making him moan, so she put a merciful inch or two between them. "We're going to the movies in Pentwater tomorrow night, Chandler. You're welcome to go with us."

We? Still holding her loosely, he eyed her with suspicion. "Not you and two hundred campers, I hope!"

That earned a throaty chuckle. "No-o-o-o, me and forty staffers. I have to chaperon them."

He let out his breath in a quiet sigh of disappointment. "Okay."

"Okay what?"

"Okay, I'll go along to the movies." Keeping one arm around her waist, he turned to walk in the direction of the rapidly vanishing flashlights. "What do we do, charter a bus?"

"You honestly don't know how we get to Pentwater?" she asked in amazement, then quickly hid her glee when he admitted that he had no idea. "Well, Chandler, don't worry about it. You'll find out tomorrow night."

She grinned to herself in the dark. Was *he* in for a surprise!

10

CHANDLER STOOD to one side of the crowd near the loading dock, regarding the truck with a slight frown. He looked, Lanni decided for the millionth time, like a first-class hunk. His crisp khaki slacks and creamy white crew-neck sweater lent him a clean-cut preppiness that seemed at odds with his dark, intriguing muscularity. Nevertheless, all his apparent contradictions added up to a man who was sexy, virile fascinating.

And evidently puzzled. "What *is* this?"

"The garbage truck," she said cheerfully.

"I recognize the garbage truck. What's it doing here?"

"See if you can figure it out."

He turned those black eyes on her, his eyebrows shooting up. "This is our chartered bus?"

She nodded and waited for his outraged reaction. He would probably refuse to go to the movies now that he'd seen their unconventional mode of transportation.

With scarcely a moment's hesitation, he shrugged off his surprise and glanced around. "Is everybody here?"

"Everyone who's going." She studied him quizzically. "We're taking the truck."

"Yeah, I got that. So are we all set?"

"I guess so." Maybe he didn't understand. "Chandler, do you honestly want to ride all the way to Pentwater in the camp garbage truck?"

His eyes narrowed just a bit. "Do you have some problem with my riding in the camp garbage truck?"

"Me? Why...no. No, of course not."

"Are you riding in it?"

"Yes."

"Then I am, too." He headed up front and opened the driver's door. "Better get your staff loaded or we'll be late for the show."

Lanni gave the order to climb aboard, then hurried after Chandler. "Do you plan to drive?"

"That's right. Any reason why I shouldn't?"

She shook her head in wry denial as she climbed up into the cab. Even if she could think of a logical reason to stop him from driving, she doubted if she'd meet with much success. The staff supervisor at Camp Ottawa was in no position to put restrictions on the board chairman at Scott-Hight.

Of course, Chandler hadn't exactly been acting much like a chairman of the board lately. He had spent a good portion of the morning trimming dead branches off the trees around the Scott cottage, assisted by Teddy Mitchell, cutting the wood up and hauling it—in the garbage truck—to the woodpile behind the eating lodge. Chandler had asked Lanni at breakfast if she would mind if Teddy helped him. Of course she'd given him permission to use the entire grounds crew if he wished, but he insisted that Teddy would be sufficient.

That afternoon he'd spent a couple of hours in Don's office, apparently going through the files, because she'd overheard him ask Don for the key to his filing cabinet. Then at supper he'd been so preoccupied she feared he would forget all about the movies. What was bothering him? Why did he keep glancing at Teddy with such a troubled look in his eyes?

She watched him shift around on the seat now to look through the rear window at the passel of teenagers in the back. When he'd assured himself that everyone was safely aboard and seated on the spare mattresses from the storage room, he jumped down from the cab and went back to lock the tailgate in place.

No, he'd definitely left his chairman-of-the-board demeanor somewhere else, she thought as he got back inside. He was behaving more like a big brother who'd found himself in charge of three dozen accident-prone younger siblings.

"Would you mind telling me how we'll know if we lose one of them?" he asked, starting the engine and putting the truck in gear.

"I'm not sure we would know, so you'd better take the bumps slowly and cross your fingers that no one bounces out." At his quick look of alarm, she chuckled. "Don't worry, Chandler. We aren't going to lose one."

"You talk as though you've done this before."

"Oh, I have! This old baby—" she patted the dashboard "—has hauled the staff to Pentwater once a month every summer for more years than I've been around. It's a sacred tradition."

He relaxed visibly. "How come I never knew anything about this so-called tradition?"

"Maybe no one thought you were the type to appreciate the cultural nature of this outing. I mean, the blue-blooded Chandler Scott going to the movies in the camp garbage truck? That would be too ironic."

His laugh sounded strange. "Well, here I am. What does that tell you about my blue blood?"

"I don't know. It might help if I knew why you're here."

I'm here because my blood is red, not blue, and I want you, just as any red-blooded man with good sense would!

He drew the truck to a halt at Sandy Lake's one stop sign. Extending his arm, he touched the tip of his index finger to her bottom lip. "I think you know why I'm here, Lanni."

His husky words, and the shocking warmth of his finger against her skin, struck a chord of fierce desire in Lanni's heart. She swallowed and turned her head just enough so the pressure of his touch increased a fraction, unaware that in doing so she sent a shaft of need lancing through Chandler.

Easy, he cautioned himself. He had to make a little contact go a long way. Last night he'd gotten carried away, and he couldn't let that happen again.

Chandler drew back his hand and shifted gears, and the truck moved on. He switched his eyes to the road and said nothing more about his reason for being there, but that didn't stop Lanni's mind from straying to the subject throughout the evening. That had been repressed hunger she'd seen in his eyes for just a moment back there—she was sure of it. Did he know what a blood-pounding attraction she felt for him?

When they parked and walked down the tree-lined block to the movie theater in Pentwater, he made sure they didn't get separated in the throng of staffers, but he did it without physically touching her. As if by magic, he kept her at his side all night. The feature film was rotten, but Lanni didn't care. Chandler wasn't complaining, either. During the movie and later, on the drive back to camp, she occasionally turned her head to find his eyes on her in the dark, the gleam in their depths compelling and totally unfathomable. He took his time about glancing away.

Whew! Her heartbeat had been rapid for the past four hours. She couldn't forget for a minute that it was Chandler sitting next to her, his broad shoulder crowding hers, his musky scent pervading the air she breathed and setting a trap for her heart. This wasn't the Chandler she'd detested for ten years, either. This was a whole new threat—a man who did nice things that he didn't want people to discover, and stumbled through an awkward apology for hurting her, and showed awesome restraint when she wished he would just make love to her instead.

This Chandler was a much bigger threat than the other one. Half of her wanted to run as far and as fast as she could, to keep from falling for him all over again. The other half was experiencing an impish urge to place her hand on his hard thigh and squeeze. She went so far as to flex her fingers and reach out through the darkness, then snatched her hand back when she realized he was speaking.

"If you don't want to tell me, just say so, Lanni."

Oops! It would appear she'd missed part of the conversation. She tried to fake it. "No, I don't mind. I was just, er, trying to remember."

"You've forgotten your husband's name?" His tone was incredulous.

"What? Of course not! His name was Tom. I mean *is* Tom. But he's my ex-husband." She recovered her composure. "Why would you want to know his name?"

"I just wondered if I knew him. You said you met him at camp."

"I did? When did I say that?"

"Just a minute ago, when I asked you."

"I couldn't have said that! I met Tom at college. He's never been west of Manhattan." She was glad he couldn't see her blush. "Maybe I wasn't exactly paying attention to what you were saying, Chandler. Was there something you wanted to ask me about Tom?"

Yeah. I'd like to know how the jerk could have let you go. Aloud he said, "I think you're too sleepy right now to make sense, Lanni. Come on—" he slid his hand beneath her hair, gently grasping her by the nape of the neck and tugging until she toppled over against him "—lay your head down and go to sleep. I'll wake you when we get back to camp."

She snuggled against him, too smart to tell him she wasn't the least bit sleepy. It was all she could do not to purr her contentment when he pressed his lips to her forehead and whispered, "We can talk tomorrow."

GIVING IN TO TEMPTATION hadn't been very wise, Chandler conceded as he walked Lanni to the door of the girls' dorm. After he'd held her close for the past twenty minutes, the very last thing he wanted was to tell her good-night and leave her. But what else could he do? Even if she had been willing, even if her responsibilities to the staff hadn't precluded her going home with him for the night, he would never again be able to assuage his hunger at her expense. His conscience wouldn't let him do that to her twice.

When they reached the porch, he cupped his hand along her jaw and tilted her face up to skim her lips with his in the only kind of kiss he dared give her—one that was swift and light and wouldn't lead to anything. He even took a chance and hugged her quickly, inhaling the delicate fragrance of her hair before releasing her.

"Good night, Lanni," he said, his voice low and indistinct.

"Night, Chandler," she said softly.

It wrenched something in his stomach to see how reluctant she seemed to go inside. From the way she lingered there just inches away from him, her palm stroking down his chest as if smoothing out imaginary wrinkles in his sweater, her eyes clinging to his face in the faint glow of the porch light, he figured maybe she didn't want him to leave, either. But at last she turned and went in.

In a way it was a relief when he could finally close the door behind her and drive back to the cottage. Not that he would be able to sleep. Knowing he had to work off some tension, he changed into cutoffs and tennis shoes and made his way down the moonlit slope to the beach. There, he set out at a quick pace along the sand, running the entire two miles of Camp Ottawa's Michigan waterfront, then turning and jogging back more slowly.

He'd run like this a lot in the past ten years, whenever he'd had trouble sleeping. If he pushed himself hard enough, the physical exertion transformed his feelings into numb exhaustion. But his troublesome thoughts usually had to be channeled in another direction. He'd never found a way to turn them off completely.

As his strong legs drove him onward, he focused his mind away from Lanni. He thought instead of what he'd learned today about Teddy Mitchell.

From the first time he saw the boy, something about him had reminded Chandler of his brother. Maybe it was his fair hair, or the fact that he was determined not to let his weakened leg slow him down. At eighteen, Scotty had given life his best shot, too, against overwhelming odds. Maybe that was why Teddy kept tugging at Chandler, making him wonder about things. Or maybe it was the elusive sadness he'd glimpsed in the kid's eyes, and the hunch that Ted's life was a big lie, just like Chandler's.

When he'd asked Don Grant two weeks ago how the Mitchell boy had hurt his leg, Don told him a story about a fall from a horse. He'd mentioned, too, other injuries, each with a perfectly plausible explanation. Nothing to make one think twice.

Only... as they worked together in the hot sun this morning, stripped to the waist and sweating, Chandler's undemanding interest seemed to touch a need in Teddy, and the boy began talking. He'd talked about everything from girls to college, and in the process he told Chandler that his leg had been broken when he fell off a second-story landing at home. Chandler asked enough seemingly offhand questions to be sure there was no horse involved in either that accident or the one when Teddy broke his arm.

His suspicions aroused, he'd called a private investigator right after lunch and asked him to look into Guy Mitchell's legal and domestic history. He'd offered a sizeable bonus if the report came before five o'clock. The P.I. called back within three hours, and his report didn't relieve Chandler's mind. It seemed that the gentleman horse farmer on Scott-Hight's board of directors had a record of numerous arrests, but no convictions, on charges of assault and battery and disorderly conduct, all committed while under the influence of alcohol. Mitchell's standing in the community, as well as the judge's belief that the man was under a great deal of stress, had contributed to the repeated dropping of charges.

The "stress" had apparently varied from arrest to arrest. One year he was in danger of losing his farm to the bank; another time a fire had destroyed his stable and seven of his best horses. Just two months before Teddy's leg had been crushed in a fall from a horse—at least that was the cause listed on the official hospital record—Mrs. Mitchell had walked out on Guy and the boy. During the following year Mitchell had hired and then fired, or otherwise couldn't keep, eleven different housekeepers. Frequently the father and son had to care for the large house themselves. The next spring Teddy ended up back in the hospital with a broken arm, which was explained away as a skating accident. Since then he'd had other "accidents," although none had resulted in fractures.

Considering that information, Chandler had a sick feeling in the pit of his stomach. Dear God, he hoped he was wrong! How could something like what he suspected go on for years without anyone noticing?

While waiting for the detective to call him back, he'd read the camp file on Teddy and had found no indication that anything was amiss. Certainly no one on the Scott-Hight board had ever suspected anything. If anyone back home in Kentucky had noticed, why didn't they report it to the authorities? But then, the local authorities hadn't seen fit to deal with Guy's tendency to get drunk under pressure and fight grown-ups. Wasn't it possible they'd have let him off the hook as well for knocking his only child around?

Some people aren't fit to be parents, he thought as he ran, turning clammy as the chilling venomous rage snaked through his veins. *Some parents aren't even human.* The hatred was a familiar acid that had corroded his soul for ten years, and he feared deep inside that it reduced him to the level of those he despised.

In an effort to stay calm, he told himself he could be wrong about Mitchell. At supper that night, and off and on since then, he'd scrutinized Teddy for some sign that would either confirm or disprove the suspicions, but the boy was very good at hiding behind a smile.

Chandler reached the lone pine tree below the cottage and slowed to a walk. Finally he stopped, breathing hard, and bent over to rest, hands on his knees. Grimly he faced the fact that he would have to talk to Teddy about this. He didn't know when or where he would broach the subject, or what he'd say, and he sure as hell didn't look forward to it, but he did know he didn't have any choice.

CHANDLER LOOKED as if he'd gotten even less sleep than Lanni, if that was possible. Studying the lines of fatigue around his mouth and eyes as he picked up her sun visor from the bottom of the sailboat and tossed it to Lanni on shore, she wondered if the same thing had kept them both awake last night.

Fantasies of what could come of this precious new friendship.

Desire, more elemental and intense than any she'd ever felt in her life.

Frustration.

Maybe that wasn't his problem, though. He didn't look aroused, he looked tired. The entire two hours they'd been on the water, he'd been so busy with the jib lines and the tiller, or whatever those things were called, that she had to wonder why he'd suggested they go for a sail. Sailing was hard work, and he needed to rest. But then he remarked that he used to sail a lot here on Sandy Lake when he came to camp with his family, and she realized he was still trying to handle his memories of Scotty and his father. That was why he'd wanted to take one of the boats out.

Since it was obvious that her knowledge of sailing was sadly lacking, he asked her how a young lady could grow up near Cape Cod and spend her summers at Camp Ottawa without at least learning the basics of tacking.

"By being a total bookworm," she said with a shrug. "At camp I always opted for nature studies or arts and crafts rather than sailing." Her eyes sparkled. "There are ways to get around it, if you're devious enough."

"Devious?" He grinned at her self-description and a moment later had her talking about her years spent in the camping program. From there he eased her into a discussion of college and her teaching career, asking just enough questions about her marriage to get the general picture of her incompatibility with Tom Preston. Since he didn't probe too deeply, Lanni found that she didn't mind his curiosity.

Watching him secure the boat and climb out to join her on the dock, she told herself that he probably respected her privacy because he guarded his own so jealously. Yet he was interested to hear about the little girl she'd been, and to discover her youthful dreams, and to know if she ever saw her ex-husband, and that discovery gave her hope. Perhaps behind that shield of respect and restraint, he actually yearned to get closer to someone.

Interesting possibility, she thought as they drove past Perry's Place and back through the arched entry gates into Camp Ottawa. As for herself, she was feeling remarkably close to Chandler, despite certain aspects of his life that puzzled her as much as ever.

When the fork in the road loomed before them, she found herself waiting anxiously to see which way he would turn—right, in the direction of Lanni's dorm, or left, toward the Scott cottage.

Chandler pulled the Pontiac to the side of the road and tried to hold back an ungallant yawn. Suddenly wondering if Lanni was going to think he was playing games, he looked over at her and met her watchful gray eyes. "Uh, Lanni, I can take you back to the dorm if you like, or you can come home with me for a while."

"You look like you need a little sleep," she observed, generously offering him an out. When he admitted that he did, she smothered a sigh of regret. "I guess I'll get on back and rest, too. Sunday afternoon's about the only time I can take a nap around here."

Tightening his hands on the wheel, he cut his eyes back to the rustic carved signposts just ahead. "There are two sofas in my living room. You can have one. I'll sleep on the other." Dammit, it did sound like a line! He exhaled impatiently. "I'm not thrilled at the idea of sharing you with two hundred kids and forty teenagers, Lanni."

It wasn't necessary to tell him the campers were cooking out on their own that day, or that the staff had the day off, too. Excitement surged through her in a joyous, uplifting wave, but she disciplined her smile and pretended for a moment to consider his announcement gravely. "You'll really stick to your own sofa?"

He nodded without looking at her. She sure didn't trust him. Not that he blamed her.

"Aw, heck! That's what I figured. Oh, well. I guess I'll go with you, anyway."

When he turned dark, startled eyes on her, she gave him a small sidelong grin that lifted a heavy weight from his shoulders. Evidently she trusted him more than he trusted himself.

By now Lanni was used to finding strange automobiles parked at the Scott cottage, so when she saw the dark gray Cadillac—probably another rental car—she experienced only a dash of surprise. "You seem to have company."

Chandler was already arming himself with caution, trying to figure out what on earth Caroline could be doing there. At least, he was reasonably sure it was Caroline.

It was. She looked right at home, which was one of the most charming things about her. When Chandler took Lanni inside, Caroline was drinking a cup of hot tea, curled up on a sofa with an unobstructed view of the water, her elegant stockinged legs tucked beneath her, but she rose at once, smiling as she extended her hand. "Hello! You must be Lanni Preston. Don's told me so many wonderful things about you. I'm Caroline Scott." She lifted her lovely blue eyes to the man who lagged a step behind Lanni. "Chandler's mother," she added softly, with unmistakable warmth.

Lanni was too delighted at meeting Mrs. Scott to realize that the afternoon wasn't going to turn out the way she had hoped. Before very long Chandler's mother had situated the two younger people at the kitchen table and was happily preparing a big pot of creamed chipped beef, the ingredients for which she'd purchased in Muskegon. "Actually I just flew in for the afternoon to make sure Chandler is eating properly. This was his favorite dish when he was growing up," she confided over her shoulder to Lanni, who felt as though she'd known the older woman for years. "He used to beg me to make it for him every Wednesday."

"Wednesday was the cook's day off," Chandler reminded Caroline with a trace of dry amusement. "And creamed beef was the only thing you knew how to fix. You'd better believe I loved it!"

"He would have asked for creamed beef even if I'd been a marvelous cook," Caroline insisted. "You should have seen how much of the stuff he could put away."

"And it just made him keep growing, didn't it?" Lanni said, admiring Chandler's muscular length. "Or have all the men in your family been this tall?"

Chandler traced a fingertip along the grain of the tabletop as he waited for Caroline to answer. "My husband was almost as tall as Chandler," the lady said thoughtfully, stirring the mixture on the stove. She reached up and smoothed a strand of pale blond hair back into its French twist. "Scotty took after me physically, I'm afraid. He was smaller and not terribly athletic."

After lunch, when Mrs. Scott got down the family albums from the living room bookshelves and began showing them to Lanni, Chandler abruptly excused himself to go clean up the dishes. He didn't care to watch while Lanni examined his baby pictures and made the inevitable comparison to Scotty and everyone else in the family. He knew damn well he didn't fit in; he didn't need her to point that out. He also feared the differences were much more than skin deep.

But, alone in the kitchen, he couldn't help wondering what they were talking about out there. And he couldn't help wishing, with the old dull ache of loneliness, that he could be with them.

11

LANNI TRIED HARD to figure out what problem Chandler had with his mother. Personally she found Caroline Scott to be irresistible—friendly, beautiful, smart and witty. It didn't take a genius to tell that she loved her son more than anything in the world, or that her sole purpose in coming to Michigan for a three-hour visit was to find out who was occupying Chandler's time there.

If Caroline had been less well-bred, less gracious and kind, she might have alienated Lanni in the process of checking her out. But she gave every indication that she approved thoroughly of Chandler's... well, his *involvement* with Lanni, if that was the correct term. Before the afternoon was over, she had diplomatically gleaned enough salient facts to be able to write a brief but credible biography about Lanni and had managed to persuade the younger woman to call her Caroline.

Chandler did have a problem, though. Even if Lanni hadn't already been convinced of that, she'd have picked up on the guarded look in his eyes and would have blamed it on more than mere nerves at having his mother meet Lanni.

But there was no doubt he loved Caroline. At five o'clock, he took Lanni aside and asked if she would mind following in his car while he drove his mother's rented car back to Muskegon for her. Lanni was glad to help. When they reached the airport and Caroline had departed for Philadelphia in her private jet, Chandler's mood actually seemed lighthearted. Good, Lanni thought. Maybe those two had straightened things out between them on the drive.

Chandler congratulated himself on making it through an encounter between Lanni and Caroline without any skeletons toppling out of his closet. Not that he'd been afraid Caroline would say too much. Experience had taught him just how well she could keep a secret. But she clearly felt he should level with Lanni. That was what she meant by her not-so-subtle comments: "She's a strong girl, Chandler. I'm glad to see your taste in women has improved," and "I like Lanni very much. She's someone I feel we can trust."

There would have been no point in his pretending not to be interested in Lanni, so he didn't even try. But neither did he intend to bare his soul to her. There was no way anything could come of this relationship. He just wanted to enjoy it while he could. When it got too risky, he'd force himself to end it.

As they set out north on U.S. 31 from Muskegon, Chandler patted the seat next to him. "Come sit over here. Help me stay awake."

She slid over and settled against him compliantly, and his pulse rate shot skyward when she put her hand on his thigh. Well, at least there was no chance he'd fall asleep. Although he'd probably go into cardiac arrest if she moved her hand any higher.

She didn't feel like sleeping, either. Too much was going on inside her suddenly hot body. She'd been enjoying the shock waves of arousal off and on all day—just one of the perks of spending time with Chandler. Those pictures Caroline had shown her of a little angel with creamy olive skin, enormous dark eyes and spiky black eyelashes, wearing not so much as a diaper on his chubby bottom, had given Lanni dangerous ideas. She'd been possessed by a crazy but powerful yearning to make a baby with Chandler—a baby that would look just like that adorable little boy in the pictures. Thinking that such totally mad impulses were certain to get her in trouble, she decided she'd better keep her hands to herself from now on.

"Hey, put that back," he ordered her when the provocative weight of her hand left his leg. Sensing her hesitation, he used an unfair tactic to persuade her. "Caroline likes you, you know."

It worked. Lanni promptly returned her hand to his heated, tensed-up thigh, wanting confirmation of what she had suspected all afternoon.

During the course of her visit, whenever Chandler was out of earshot, Caroline had confided all sorts of information about him, revealing little points of motherly pride. How on graduation from Harvard he'd refused all help from her and Chandler, Sr., preferring to roughneck in the Texas oil fields, earning calluses on his hands and saving his money to start his own business, which was by now an unqualified success. How he'd completely renovated an old farmhouse near Dallas and landscaped the four-acre tract, planning and executing every last detail of the work himself in his spare time. That was where he lived, quietly, alone. How he'd taken classes at the University of Texas at Arlington to acquaint himself with not just the language but the history and culture of Mexico. And how since his father died he'd started spending several days each month in Philadelphia with Caroline, seeing to her business matters and arranging for the upkeep of her property. His advice meant far more than that of all her lawyers and business managers.

Lanni had been deeply touched by Caroline's shared confidences. She certainly hoped Chandler was right about his mother's opinion of her. "You don't think she's put off by my occupation?"

"Teaching art? Why should that bother her?"

"Not teaching," Lanni corrected him. "Cleaning johns."

"Oh, that occupation. Is that how you would describe your work at camp?"

"Well, it is within my jurisdiction. Has you mother ever in her life cleaned a toilet?"

"Not to my knowledge, but I'm sure she understands that someone has to do the job."

"And better me than her, right?"

He coughed behind one hand, hiding his grin. "I think you underestimate Caroline. She's not a snob. There's nothing in this world she won't do for someone she loves."

"And she does love you." Shifting his shoulders in sudden uneasiness, he nodded, and after a moment's consideration, Lanni said under her breath, "I guess I

have more in common with Caroline than I thought."
She sounded surprised.

Chandler glanced quickly at her, afraid to ask what
she meant. He had a terrible sinking feeling that she was
starting to care too much. *That* was what she had in
common with Caroline.

Lanni wasn't much happier with the discovery than
he was. *Oh, Mercer,* she thought with an inner groan,
you've let yourself get in too deep! You love that man.

She should have realized it that afternoon, when
she'd discovered that every little thing about him appealed to her . . . the tiny laugh lines fanning out from
the corners of his dark eyes; his unfailing good man-
ners that strived to make her feel comfortable with
Caroline; the oddly vulnerable look on his face when
he enfolded his mother in a hug at the airport and kissed
her goodbye. Lanni had wanted to hold him close then,
too, to smooth away the lines that suddenly grooved
his forehead and cheeks, to kiss away the sadness from
his usually sensual mouth. That should have clued her
in, that her emotions were getting way out of hand.
That, plus the profound admiration she felt whenever
she thought of the man he had become. She should have
recognized her feelings before now. She ought to have
done something—anything—to keep herself from falling for Chandler Scott. He might have changed in many
ways, but he still wasn't safe to love.

But Lanni acknowledged that she couldn't possibly
have stopped the deep, intense feelings once they
started growing. No matter what black secrets Chan-

dler harbored in his heart, she loved him. Not that she could tell him so.

As they swept across the Sandy Lake bridge and turned toward Camp Ottawa, Chandler reached up to rub the back of his neck. What was he going to do when he reached that fork in the road? Take Lanni to her dorm? That was the safer route—for both of them—but an intrinsically selfish part of him rebelled at making such a sacrifice.

"You never got that nap," she said softly.

He gave her a searching look. "Neither did you."

Her expression innocent, she yawned and stretched in a highly provocative way. "I know." Her tone was wistful. "The campers are cooking out tonight, and the staff are having a party at the lodge, so I don't have anyone to supervise. Of course, we could always drop by and say hello to the kids if you like."

"Is that what you want to do?"

Lanni hesitated, then decided that beating around the bush was not her style. "No. I'd rather go home with you and help myself to some more of that creamed chipped beef and—" she grinned "—other things."

Food and sleep, Chandler thought as he took the left branch in the road at the signpost. That was all he was offering her. Some mutually gratifying company and a place to relax.

Ha! If that was all there was to this, then why was he having so much trouble breathing all of a sudden?

LANNI PUSHED AWAY her plate of half-eaten food. "I guess I wasn't as hungry as I thought."

Chandler nodded. He hadn't been able to eat much, either. Just as he hadn't been able to stop looking at her. The first couple of times she'd intercepted his stare, she gave him a smile that he felt all the way to his toes, but for the past few minutes she just looked right back at him, her eyes smoky, her tongue tracing delicately back and forth across her bottom lip. She appeared to be rather warm, too, which was a mild way to describe Chandler's body temperature.

He cleaned off the table, moving slowly to give him time to think. What now?

"Nap?" she asked from just behind him, and he swung around to face her. Had she been reading his mind? He inhaled, breathed in her delicious scent and felt his knees weaken. "Nap," she said decisively, seeing the desire flare in his eyes.

Chandler convinced himself they really were going to sleep. When she bypassed the sofas and headed upstairs, he told himself it made sense. Beds were made for sleeping. When she opened his bedroom door and led the way in, he came to a stop in the doorway, tilted his head back and watched her through hooded eyes.

Lanni moved over and sat down on his bed, then leaned back on both elbows in a way that emphasized her curves in the cotton blouse and tight jeans. She looked long and lithe and totally feminine, her hair spilling in a cascade of rich chestnut silk over one shoulder and pooling on the patchwork quilt where she lay.

He could feel the stuttering rhythm of his pulse as a hungry fire began to crawl along his veins. Drawing another deep, unsteady breath, he began to back up. "I'll take the bedroom next door."

"I wish you wouldn't."

Her soft words stopped him. He glanced back at her warily, finally forced to acknowledge that she was seducing him. The glimmer in her eyes hinted at a need that matched his. Her languorous pose was sexy, irresistible. It set his blood to pounding, rushing to his head.

Unsmiling, he turned to face her squarely. "Lanni, I thought we were beyond playing games with each other."

"I'm not playing games. I'd really rather share a room with you than have you next door."

"Why?" At the look on her face, he gestured impatiently with one hand. "Okay, never mind. I retract the question."

"I should hope so! Lord, Chandler, we're both adults. Whenever you're around, I sense a lot of, mmm, sexual tension between us." His ironic grimace conceded the truth of that. She stood up and looked straight into his eyes. "You told me once to let you know when I decided to be honest with myself. So now I'm ready to admit it. I want to make love with you."

She didn't know what reaction she'd expected from Chandler, but it wasn't the one she got. He shook his head and came over to drop heavily onto the side of the bed. Propping his elbows on his knees, he bent his head and plunged his fingers into his black hair. "Haven't I apologized enough, Lanni?" he asked with a groan. "Do you have to keep reminding me how I hurt you?"

She stared at him in surprise. "I don't want another apology. I'm trying to tell you, you were right. From the morning I saw you lying naked and asleep on this bed, I've been unable to ignore the way you make me feel. And believe me, I've tried to ignore it. But the feelings have only grown stronger." She sat down beside him, her thigh pressing warmly against his. "I got the impression that first day that you wanted me, too. Was I wrong?"

His fingers dug into his thick hair. "You know damn well I want you! It hurts like hell that I can't let myself touch you the way I'd like."

Her slender hand slid over to rest on his upper leg, and she heard his indrawn breath. "Lanni, stop it!" he rasped, pushing her hand away. "No games, please! I've apologized. I've admitted I want you. What more can I do?"

"You can pay attention to what I'm saying, and then believe it. I want to love you. Today. Now."

His head jerked back and forth. "No, Lanni. I used you once. It was a mistake I'm not going to make again."

Exasperation made her want to grab his suitcase and smash it over his obstinate head. But that, she reasoned, wouldn't exactly set the mood for romance.

When she cupped her palm against the back of his neck, every muscle in his body coiled tight in response. Her fingertips began trailing through the black satin curls on his nape with a light, tantalizing touch that immobilized him. Lanni leaned toward him and kissed his hand, the side of his head, his wrist, his throat, and he sat through it all, unable to protest.

"Ten years ago it was a mistake," she whispered close to his ear. "We didn't know what love was all about." She ran her tongue down his forearm, then laved the smooth bronze skin on the inside of his elbow. Shuddering, he unclenched his fingers from his hair, then sat up straight to stare at the wall. She reached for his hand and laced her fingers through his, bringing them up to her mouth and planting a lingering, heated kiss on the back of his knuckles. "Now I know what I'm doing, Chandler. And I know I love you."

He squeezed his eyes shut and tried not to feel her kisses. They were playing sneaky tricks on his mind. He couldn't think straight when she let her hands and lips wander so freely over his body. "You thought you loved me the last time, remember? Lanni, don't waste yourself on me. I'm not who you think. You called it right that first day. I'm a bastard. I can't give you what you need."

Her free hand moved up to shield his thudding heart, her thumb stroking over the muscled wall of his chest, tracing his shape. She tilted her head and nuzzled his jaw. "I'm not asking for your undying devotion, Chandler. I've grown up since the last time. You don't have to love me even a little bit. All I ask is that you don't deny what I feel. Just trust me. And please, Chandler, let me give you my love. It won't hurt, I promise."

Maybe it was because he was so tired, but crazy ideas were starting to make sense to him, and wrong suddenly looked temptingly right.

He managed a rough laugh at the absurdity of her plea, then caught her to him and pressed her face to his chest. "Hurt? Oh, Lord help me, Lanni, it'll only hurt when you stop." He held her there for a moment, both of them barely breathing, then rubbed his cheek against the lush softness of her hair and kissed the top of her head with what felt almost like a sigh. "Okay, babe. I'm not strong enough to say no."

He lifted his head and gazed at her with a rueful half smile. This might be the second biggest mistake he'd ever made with Lanni, but he lacked the willpower to leave before he committed it.

He stood up slowly. "I'd better have a shower." He headed for the bathroom, then paused and looked back at her. "Or you can have the bathroom first."

"I have a better idea." She rose, too, and moved toward him, her hands reaching for his clothes.

Lanni had known what she would find when she unbuttoned the blue-striped, short-sleeved shirt and stripped it off Chandler's broad shoulders. She had made numerous mental lists of his many outstanding physical attributes—his incredible muscles and the gleaming, sun-bronzed darkness of his skin, the small flat copper-colored nipples waiting tautly for her touch, the dusting of fine black hair on his chest that tapered down to an arrow before disappearing into the waistband of his jeans. Her deft fingers, when they unfastened his Levi's and tugged them down past his hips, uncovered no surprises. Even when they trembled and turned shy on her at the task of removing his jockey shorts, she knew what treasures would be revealed.

What she had forgotten—what she'd never fully realized at nineteen—was the way his body would feel all naked and exposed and *beautiful.* Now she reveled in his texture, stroking her hands with wonder down the damp, musky warmth of his skin.

He was all hard bone and firm muscle, smooth in places and rough in others. It was like touching a primitive power that had taken the awesome form of a god. And he felt so vibrantly, so humanly alive! His breath escaped in ragged spurts, his chest heaved, his heat seared her palms, and his manhood . . . oh, mercy, his manhood.

Lanni's hand skated down past his rib cage to his abdomen before Chandler stopped it. "Not yet," he said huskily and began undressing her.

Halfway through, he had to pause a moment, to cross his arms on his chest and tuck his hands beneath his armpits in order not to rush things. His first impulse had been to rip away her clothes, to see everything at once, but he knew this was going to be over much too soon as it was. He needed to make it last.

Black eyes glowing, he studied her peaches-and-cream body, bare from the waist up. Her breasts were exquisite, shapely and firm and just the right size to fit into his palm, if he ever allowed himself that luxury. Tall and reed slim, her chestnut hair a cloud of silk floating around her shoulders, her smoky eyes on his face, she waited with unguarded anticipation for his next move.

Steady, old boy, he told himself, his humor strained. *Slow and easy.*

He uncrossed his arms and reached for her waist. Undid her jeans. Drew them gently, gently, down her legs, his hands skimming the satin lengths. Carefully he supported her as he extracted one foot at a time from her trousers. Then he returned his hands to her hips and repeated the process with her lacy bikini briefs. He sucked in a long draft of air and stared.

She was more beautiful than he'd imagined, and his mind had been pretty creative when he thought about this. Her curves were subtle yet distinct enough to satisfy his discriminating eye. Her arms and legs were lightly tanned from the summer sun. She had a creamy soft look about her that he knew was real, tactile. Her delicate face possessed a calm clear-eyed beauty that had appealed to him from the first time he saw her weeks earlier, but now it shone with a tender warmth that had never been there before. She couldn't possibly have looked this good ten years ago. Even so—even considering his reasons for needing to forget—it seemed impossible that he could have forgotten her.

He pulled her close in a fierce hug, then stifled a groan of need as her silk-skinned fragility aroused every nerve that she came in contact with. Intensely pleasurable sensations swept over him and he clung to her, rotating his hips against hers incautiously. His desire escalated.

Now it was Lanni who slowed them down. "Chandler," she said breathlessly, "weren't we going to take a shower?" His mouth to her throat, he murmured, "I don't know. Were we?"

She nodded and wriggled loose. He gave her a regretful look but followed her to the bathroom and stepped into the tub with her without complaining. She turned on the spray, adjusted the temperature, reached for the soap and began to lather them both up as best she could with Chandler standing an inch away, neither helping nor interfering. He didn't move at all, in fact, except to make sure Lanni didn't get any farther away than that meager inch.

As far as showers went, it was probably the best one she'd ever experienced. Chandler enjoyed it, too, if the sounds he made deep in his throat when she soaped him up were any indication. She might not have minded staying there the rest of the evening, sudsing and rinsing and then testing to be sure he was squeaky clean, but she grew impatient for more. Finally she shut off the water, grabbed a couple of towels and did a hasty job of drying herself. Chandler still seemed content to let her do as she pleased with his body, and she slowed down to rub the bath towel over his healthy brown limbs and torso.

He was, she noticed with fluttering pulse, a perfect physical specimen. And the shower hadn't diminished his arousal one iota.

"Would you hurry up?" he asked in a low, controlled voice when she had dried his front for the third time.

"It's this towel," she excused herself. "It's too small. I just wanted to be sure you were dry."

"I'm dry," he said, having evidently tolerated her enticing ministrations as long as possible. "If I were any dryer, I couldn't walk." She didn't even have to look again to see what he meant; she could feel it, as close as she was standing to him.

He placed both hands on her shoulders and turned her, guiding her over the edge of the bathtub, down the hall to the bedroom and straight to the bed. Sliding his arms around her waist, he pulled her close and kissed her slowly, then with increasing fervor as the friction of their bodies rubbing together sharpened all their senses. The sweetness of her mouth seemed to invite exploration, and his tongue plunged in hungrily for a taste.

Lanni's fingers kneaded his back as the passion swelled within her. She'd never been so aware of the nerves just below the surface of her skin. But Chandler had ignited a wildfire that had spread to every nerve, every last cell of feeling in her being. The fire penetrated deep into her bones and made her burn with want of him. She moaned and tried to pull him closer, and when his lips left her mouth and trailed flaming kisses down the side of her throat to her breasts, she arched her back and cried out his name.

"I love you, Chandler Scott," she said, her breath catching on a sob. "But if you don't stop torturing me, I'm going to murder you!"

"Do you really want me to stop?" he whispered as his tongue circled one nipple and his lips teased the dusky rosebud mercilessly.

"Yes. No! Oh, Chandler, just love me before I die from needing you."

"Mmm, why didn't you just say so?"

The next thing she knew, they were lying together on the bed, arms and legs tangled. His long, muscular thigh parted hers and he eased down to her with a gentle strength that didn't surprise her. She might not know all there was to know about this man who hid so much of himself behind locked doors and silence, but she knew he had a great capacity to love and a tender reluctance to hurt someone he cared about.

He kissed the corner of her mouth. "All right, honey?"

Smiling, she lifted her hips up toward his. "More than all right. *Desperate!*"

His fingers wove into her tousled silk hair and soothingly massaged her temples as he lowered himself the final inch necessary to fuse them together. She received his throbbing male strength with a rush of deep feeling. Her hands grasped his buttocks to show him that she wanted him to stay there, that he wasn't hurting her.

Lord, she loved him! She told him so with words and in a dozen unspoken ways as he rocked against her. His hungry heart absorbed all that she offered, and he responded with rising passion, murmuring sweet things in her ear, thrusting as far as he could into her secret core, as though this was the only way he knew to reach in and take hold of her love.

Chandler felt driven, carried beyond every limit he'd ever passed before. His intense desire was the raging inferno that fueled his flight, but an almost overwhelming tenderness made the trip worthwhile. He wanted to cling to Lanni and carry her with him to whatever exciting new realm he was rushing toward. But at the back of his mind, he remembered that this was only a moment, no matter how perfect, and that when it ended he would be alone again.

Just enjoy it, he cautioned himself, and then he forgot to worry about how long he would have her with him, because in one blinding instant it seemed as if they had become just one person, two souls united in one body, floating lightly through space, surrounded by stars and held in the grip of a hundred thousand unbelievable sensations.

THEY MADE LOVE AGAIN, this time with a wonder and appreciation for each other that neither had ever experienced before. Lanni had a glowing sense of well-being that she hadn't felt since she was a kid waking up on Christmas morning. On top of that, she discovered that loving Chandler did peculiar things to her appetite. Suddenly she was starving, and wide awake, as well.

Getting dressed, they went back downstairs and finished off Caroline's creamed beef, and still Lanni was hungry. "You know what I'd like?" Her eyes sparkled.

Chandler made a guess, which earned him a reproachful look from her. "I never realized what dirty minds you board chairmen have. No, Mr. Scott, while your suggestion does sound rather intriguing, I was talking about a hamburger. I'd love a big, juicy burger from Perry's Place."

"Followed by...dessert?" he asked, his eyebrows wiggling meaningfully.

"Definitely," she agreed.

Twilight blanketed the woods as they drove through camp, and they were almost upon the running figure before they saw it. Chandler slammed on his brakes and the girl stumbled and fell to her knees at the edge of the road.

Denise! What was she doing there, looking as if she'd been crying? All thoughts of food and other pleasures fled as Lanni jumped out of the car and reached for the girl, pulling her to her feet. "What's wrong, Denise? Where are you going?"

"Thank heaven I found you," Denise said, gasping for breath. "I've been looking all over for you."

"What's the matter?" Lanni asked again.

"It's awful!" Denise started to shake. "You've got to hurry! He's going to hurt himself—"

"Who?"

"Teddy. He's—" Denise glanced at Chandler, who had joined them beside the car, his dark attention riveted on her and Lanni.

Lanni's voice was sharp, urgent. "He's *what*, Denise?"

The girl moaned softly, afraid of getting Teddy into trouble. But even greater was her fear for the boy's life.

She swallowed. "He's drunk. And he's taken some pills, some pain pills that he keeps for when his leg hurts bad. I don't know how many he took. I tried to make him give me the rest, but he wouldn't. He said—" Her voice quavered and tears filled her eyes. "He said he wants to die!"

Lanni maintained a calm facade, but inside she was quaking, more scared than she'd ever been in her entire life. If they were too late . . . if anything happened to Teddy . . . oh, God, she couldn't even let herself contemplate it!

"Where—" she began, but Chandler firmly set her aside and interrupted, addressing Denise. "Where is he?" He was already pushing the girl into the front seat of his car, obviously expecting Lanni to be smart enough to get inside, too.

"The boys' dorm. When he didn't show up for our party this evening, I went looking for him. I found him a little while ago, and I was afraid to leave him but I knew I had to get help."

Chandler slammed the door behind Lanni, then went around and got into the driver's seat and started the engine. "Where's Don?"

"At the campers' cookout on the beach, I think." Denise sniffed and wiped her eyes.

The tires screeched as he took off to find Teddy. His eyes were fixed grimly on the road as he drove. "Lanni, take this car on to Perry's Place and telephone for an ambulance." A couple of minutes later he parked at the boys' dorm and pulled Denise out the door after him, then spoke over his shoulder to Lanni, who was sliding over to drive. "When you're sure the paramedics are on the way, go find Don."

IT WAS A NIGHTMARE. It had to be. Teddy couldn't have intentionally tried to hurt himself. Lanni watched the emergency medical technicians load the boy into the ambulance, saw his flushed face and limp form, and desperately held back a sob. *Please, God, don't let him die!*

Chandler climbed in back with Teddy and knelt on the floor next to him like a dark guardian angel that refused to be left behind. Chandler's rigid mask betrayed nothing, but his expressive eyes told Lanni just how hard he was taking this. They were full of the same fear and anguish that Lanni felt, but other emotions burned in their depths as well—bitter guilt and barely contained fury.

Why? Why guilt and anger?

Don stood next to Lanni as the ambulance pulled away. "I ought to call his father."

She agreed that Mr. Mitchell probably ought to know. But they'd both heard Teddy's groggy plea a few minutes earlier: "Don't tell Dad. Please, Chandler. Not about this." And they'd heard Chandler's gruff promise.

"Teddy's eighteen years old," she reminded Don, her voice husky with tears. "He's an adult. If he doesn't want to tell his father, we should respect that."

Don sighed. "You're right. Besides, we don't even know how serious it is." He glanced at Denise, who was being comforted by several of her friends. "One of us needs to get the staff together and calm everyone down. They're all in shock."

"I can't even calm myself down." Lanni ran her fingers through her long, tousled hair, pushing it back from her face and then brushing away the dampness from her cheeks. "Don, would you mind very much handling that?"

"You want to go to the hospital?" She nodded, not trusting her voice, and he hugged her. "All right, honey. Take Chandler's car, and drive carefully. It won't help Teddy if you have an accident on the way."

She found Chandler alone outside the hospital intensive care unit and stood watching him a moment, reluctant to let him know she was there. He slumped in the chair, his eyes closed, his face unguarded and wearing such a shattered look that for a second she was afraid Teddy hadn't survived the trip to Muskegon. But if that was the case, the ER nurse wouldn't have told Lanni they'd transferred Teddy to ICU, would she?

Hesitantly she crossed the room and sat down beside him. "How is he?"

Startled, Chandler opened his eyes and sat up, rubbing his jaw with the back of his knuckles. When he was sure he had his features under control, he met her worried gaze. "They think he'll make it."

She felt fresh tears well up in her eyes. "Thank God!"

He nodded shortly and looked away, trying to swallow the baseball-size lump in his throat.

"Did they pump his stomach?"

Although Chandler cleared his throat, his voice came out hoarse. "No. The drug had already had time to get into his bloodstream when we got here."

"Then how—" she choked over the question "—how can they be sure he's out of danger?"

"They can't. That's why he's in the ICU—so they can watch him tonight."

"But you said—"

"I said they think he'll live," he corrected her flatly. "They're pretty sure he didn't take much Demerol, because the bottle was still nearly full, and because he didn't pass out until the ambulance got there. He'd just had enough beer to exacerbate the effects of the drug."

"I see," she said slowly, searching his face. "Do you believe he'll be okay?"

As he stared out the window at the darkness, a muscle in his cheek twitched and moisture gathered at the corner of his eye. "I think he'll live, yes."

Suddenly his meaning hit her. "But something's really wrong, isn't it? He really wanted to die."

He didn't answer, just swallowed again, painfully, and tried to make the tears vanish by sheer willpower. When that didn't work, he rose to his feet and moved over to the window, to pretend to study the night outside.

He didn't know she'd followed him until her smooth, warm hand touched his arm and tugged, trying to make him face her. He refused. "Chandler," she said softly, "look at me."

Instead, he bent his head and looked down at her hand. A solitary tear landed with a splat on her creamy skin, and he quickly reached over and scrubbed it away.

"Don't look so embarrassed," she scolded him with a sniff. "That was mine, not yours."

He lifted his head in confusion. "Yours?"

"I'm crying, too. You're not the only one who cares about Teddy, you know."

When she slid both hands around his waist and wrapped him in a hard, tight hug, something gave way inside him. His arms enfolded her and he buried his damp face in the curve of her neck, nosing into her hair.

"Don't fight it," she whispered, and he found himself listening. "There's nothing unmanly about crying."

Her words mesmerized him—her words and the way she felt against him. She was so soft, so warm and supple. She was the strength he needed, and he held on to her with a quiet desperation that continued even after his eyes dried. Lord, he wished he would never have to give her up!

Lacing his brown fingers into the silken length of her hair, he rubbed his palm slowly down her back, then drew a deep shuddering breath and pushed her gently away.

Lanni lifted her eyes to the man she loved and vowed to make him as glad about her love as she suddenly was. Only maybe this wasn't the right moment.

"How do we help Teddy?" she asked softly.

To her surprise, guilt clouded his eyes. He turned away, his shoulders hunched. "Oh, God, Lanni, this is all my fault."

"What's all your fault?"

"I've suspected for weeks that he had real problems. Yesterday I uncovered enough evidence that I should have seen this coming. I should have tried to head it off."

She stared at his erect back. "What kind of evidence?"

Sighing, he pivoted and leaned back against the wall, thrusting his hands into his pockets. With his eyes focused on a spot just beyond her, he told her what he knew about Teddy's relationship with his father. As Lanni listened, she fitted it all in with her own impressions about Teddy.

Just imagine—the kid had held that terrible secret inside himself all the time Lanni had known him! Imagine the pain he'd endured alone, and the way he'd defended his father to everyone, making up stories to prove he was loved.

"You think that's why he took the pills with all that beer he was drinking?" One broad shoulder rose and fell in a gesture of tired affirmation, and she shook her head. "It's awful, Chandler. It breaks my heart to think of it. But I don't understand why you say it was your fault."

"Because I intended to talk to him, but I put it off." His voice held bitter self-accusation. "I didn't know what to say."

"Chandler, I've tried to talk to him, several times in fact, and he wouldn't let me close enough." She rubbed her forehead in an effort to erase the tension. "He knows we love him. Maybe he just wasn't ready to talk. And now . . . maybe now he will be. We'll see that he gets the help he needs."

He nodded, his eyes glinting with an expression that frightened Lanni. "You're thinking about his father, aren't you?" she asked, and he nodded again. "What do you plan to do about him?"

"I'd like to kill him with my bare hands." She believed him. "People who take their frustrations out on their kids sure as hell don't deserve to walk around free. What kind of parent hurts his own kid?"

He had the same introverted, harassed look that sometimes came over him at the mention of his own family, and Lanni felt a flash of horror, which she quickly denied. Even if he did sound as if he spoke from personal experience, she couldn't believe for a minute that Chandler, Sr., or Caroline Scott had ever abused him! It was preposterous.

She shook her head to scatter such nonsense. "People who hurt their kids like that are sick."

"Yeah." He pushed away from the wall abruptly and took her arm. "Come on, let's have a cup of coffee before you go back to camp."

"I'm not leaving," she said reasonably as they took the elevator up to the cafeteria. "Not until we know Teddy's going to be all right."

"That won't be until tomorrow, Lanni. Do you really want to spend the night in a hospital waiting room?"

She pursed her lips and studied him through narrowed eyes, remembering a similar conversation they'd had about the camp garbage truck. "Do you have a problem with my spending the night here?"

He almost smiled, and she knew he remembered, too. "No, I don't have a problem with it."

"Good, because I'm staying."

Neither one of them got any sleep that night. For several hours, Chandler and Lanni alternately drank gallons of black coffee and insulted the designer of the wretchedly uncomfortable chairs in the waiting room.

"Whoever he or she was must have possessed a well-padded anatomy," Lanni commented, rubbing her numb rear end as she jumped up to pace the floor. "They didn't believe in cushioning things for the rest of us."

Chandler knelt on the seat of one chair and leaned over the back, searching for the label. "Uh-huh. I thought so. Manufactured by the Marquis de Sade." He straightened and turned to settle back into the chair. Patting his lap, he looked at Lanni with warm laughter in his eyes. "How about if I provide the padding for you?"

She glanced in both directions down the hall, then gave a shrug. What did she care if anyone walked in on them? The hospital ought to have better facilities for those who had to wait.

The balance of the night proved much more pleasant than the first half had been, although Lanni still couldn't work up much enthusiasm for sleep. The closest she came to dropping off was when Chandler's bewitching left hand worked its way underneath her blouse and all but hypnotized her with the slow soothing pattern of its caresses on her sensitized skin. When she closed her eyes and snuggled deeper into his arms, she felt him fidget beneath her and wondered drowsily why he didn't seem to be as relaxed as she was.

Chandler told himself several times he should have insisted that Lanni return to camp. Then he moved his hand across the warm satin skin of her stomach and inhaled her feminine scent, and all the reasons why she shouldn't be there suddenly evaporated from his steamed-up brain. When she halfheartedly suggested that he must be tired of holding her, he silenced her with the subtle pressure of his mouth on hers.

Around sunrise, a nurse came out of the ICU and froze in midstride to stare at the two of them as if they were actually doing what Chandler had been fantasizing about for three hours.

Lanni yawned and gave the nurse an unruffled smile. Chandler's smile, although a bit sheepish, nevertheless knocked the socks off the woman. Her scowl faded and she self-consciously smoothed her uniform. "Are you here for the Mitchell boy?"

They got to their feet at once. "Yes, we are," Chandler said. "How is he?"

"He's awake, and the doctor has already checked him over this morning. One of you may go in to see him for a few minutes. Just one of you."

Lanni wanted to see Teddy, but judging from Chandler's face, she could tell he needed to see the boy. "You go in," she told him quietly, and he squeezed her hand before following the nurse.

Half an hour later he came back out looking somber, and Lanni reached up and traced the lines of weariness that bracketed his mouth. He turned his face just enough to kiss the palm of her hand, his liquid eyes holding hers, melting her heart. The embers of an old fire flickered to life in her loins.

While they were still standing there, silent and rapt, Don arrived. They broke apart slowly and turned to the camp business manager, and Chandler updated them both on Teddy's condition. The boy should remain in the hospital another day at least, but he wouldn't suffer any permanent effects of his medication overdose. There was no need to notify his father just yet.

Don listened silently, then gave a nod of relief. "I'm here to take over the waiting room, so you can go get some rest. You both look terrible. I'll bet you didn't get a wink of sleep last night, did you?" Lanni's eyes met Chandler's. She grinned and he shrugged. "So find yourselves a quiet bed somewhere and crash," Don instructed them firmly. "Everything's under control back at camp. Jack Mills will handle the staff quite well, I'm sure, and you'd be proud of the kids. They're all anxious for Teddy to get well and come back so they can show him how much they care."

Five minutes later Chandler sat behind the steering wheel of the white Pontiac, looking over at Lanni. "You want to go back to camp?"

Her lowered lashes hid the glow in her lambent eyes, the reflection of the fire that still burned inside her. "You'll never make it that far. You heard Don—you look terrible."

One corner of his mouth twitched. "Just how far do you think I can manage to drive?"

She looked down the street. "To the Holiday Inn if we're lucky."

Following her gaze, he caught sight of the motor hotel a block away. Slowly, with thundering heart and the hope that he wasn't dreaming, he nodded.

There was no hesitation as they undressed and came together in a beautifully choreographed ballet of passion. Chandler's hands, his mouth, his entire body cherished Lanni with exquisite skill, and she responded by caressing him to the point of heart-in-throat anticipation.

He whispered a plea for her to be kind, to finish him off. She kissed him in places that screamed silently for mercy. He slid his way into her center, and she felt her love grow to embrace his fullness. When he, all rough and hard and musky, lost himself in her sweet softness, the darkened room exploded into starlight and moonglow, and neither cared that it was morning outside.

"Lanni."

He spoke her name because he liked the sound of it, because it reminded him that she was real, and because he wondered if she was awake. She hadn't moved in so long that he thought she'd probably already dozed off.

She made small, drowsy, contented noises and tightened her arms around his waist. "Go back to sleep, Chandler."

He peered at her face in the dimness, so close to his own that he felt the warm mist of her breath on his cheek. "I haven't been asleep," he said.

"You haven't! You should have been. What are you waiting for?"

What he was waiting for was some kind of guarantee that Lanni would be there when he awoke. That he wouldn't discover this had all been just a dream.

When he seemed reluctant to answer her question, Lanni reached up and laid her palm along his jaw. "Are you worried about Teddy?"

Chandler's throat tightened. He didn't want to think about Teddy Mitchell, because he knew where that would lead him. He didn't want all that bitterness to surface now, with Lanni.

He swallowed and pressed his forehead against hers, his hands gripping her slender waist. He could think of nothing safe to say.

"Chandler, you talked to him this morning, didn't you? Did Teddy admit that his father hurt him?"

"Yeah." He cleared his throat. "His leg was broken when Guy knocked him down the stairs in a fit of drunken anger. I think Teddy was relieved to finally talk about it. But he kept making excuses for his father. He doesn't want Mitchell to get in trouble."

"Do you blame him? Chandler, we're talking about his father!"

He refrained from telling her what punishments he'd dreamed up for his own father in the past ten years.

"Relax, honey." He kissed her forehead. "I don't really care what happens to Guy Mitchell at this point. My main concern is the boy. I intend to make sure his father never lays a hand on him again."

"How?"

"Teddy starts college this fall. I'll see to it that he attends a school as far from home as possible and gets into a counseling program. And I'll have a talk with Mitchell. Let him know he's been found out."

"Do you plan to remove him from the Scott-Hight board?"

"Not necessarily. That gives me some leverage over his behavior." He shifted restlessly. "Are you hungry?"

"I should be, but I'm not. I'd rather stay right here and sleep twenty-four hours than go eat. How about you—are you hungry?"

He shook his head. He didn't want to move, either. And as far as he was concerned, they'd already done too much talking.

His right hand moved up to her breast and cupped it. "I'm not hungry for food, at least," he said, his voice low, his thumb provoking her nipple until she squirmed against him and forgot all about sleeping.

Lanni laughed and turned a little so her pelvis fitted against his. Feeling his knee nudge in between her legs, she ran her hands up his smoothly muscled back and hugged him warmly. "You seem to have a voracious appetite, my love."

"For you, yes. Who can blame me?"

She kissed his throat. "Don't look at me. I don't blame you for anything. I think you're perfect."

PERFECT. Lanni Mercer Preston, of the forgiving heart and loving nature, thought Chandler Scott was perfect.

He made love to her again, with a fierce desperation that failed to silence the battle in his head.

She only thinks that because she doesn't really know you. She doesn't have any idea who you are.

I could tell her.

No! It has to end soon, anyway. Let her keep her illusions.

But I don't want it to end.

What did you plan to do, marry her? You think she'd want you if she knew the truth?

So I won't tell her. If I asked her now, she'd marry me.

You'd do that to her? You are a bastard, aren't you?

No, he wouldn't do that to her. He loved her too much. Lord help him, he loved her. He should never have let things go this far.

She had fallen asleep again in his arms. He touched his mouth to her cheek and squeezed his eyes shut to hold back the tears. Lanni had said it was okay for a man to cry, but then she didn't know what he was crying about. She would change her opinion of him when she woke up.

THE MOTEL ROOM was darker than ever when Lanni awoke, which told her there was no daylight remaining outside. But she didn't need light in order to tell that she was alone in bed. She'd awakened alone too many times not to recognize the feel of it.

She propped herself up on one elbow and called out softly. "Chandler?"

There was no response. A chill of premonition climbed her spine.

Maybe he'd gone to the restaurant. He must have been starving. Or the hospital. Maybe he'd gone to check on Teddy.

Scrambling out of bed, she ran to the window and parted the drapes enough to see outside. The rented Pontiac was still parked where he'd left it, so he couldn't be far away. Light-headed with relief, she flipped on the lamp and walked back to the bed. On the table beside it lay the car keys and a large amount of cash.

Lanni didn't like the thoughts that stormed her brain. He couldn't have skipped out. Not after yesterday and this morning! He wouldn't have done that to her again.

Well, he sure hadn't left behind any other trace of himself.

She pulled her clothes on hastily, trying to believe he was waiting for her in the motel restaurant. He wasn't. So maybe he'd intended for her to pay the motel bill and drive to the hospital to meet him. But he'd paid for the room when he checked them in that morning. Just to be sure, she asked at the desk and was told that the account was all taken care of and that, no, there was no message for Lanni Preston.

Bewildered, she drove the short distance to the hospital and found Don Grant sitting by himself in the cafeteria, drinking coffee. "Where's Chandler?" she asked without preamble.

Don looked surprised. "Didn't he tell you? He's gone back to Dallas."

She sank down into a chair, her stomach churning. "Why?"

The tightness of her voice alarmed Don. "Why, he . . . he said his vacation's over, that he doesn't have any more time to play."

Play! Was that what he'd been doing?

"He saw Teddy again before he left, to tell him goodbye," Don added.

She tried to regain control of her quivering chin. "How is Teddy?"

"Much better. He's been moved to a regular room, and I'm taking him back to camp tomorrow morning. You can see him if you like."

She nodded, fighting tears. "When did you say Chandler left?"

"Early afternoon. I took him to the airport about one o'clock."

This was the hardest question she'd ever been forced to ask, and she silently cursed Chandler for making her ask it. "Did he leave any message for me?"

Don's kind heart rebelled at having to answer, but he couldn't lie. "No. I'm sorry, Lanni. But he did leave the car for you. I asked if he wanted to return it to the rental agent, but he said you might want to use it."

Oh, terrific! He left her a car and a wad of cash. She was really coming up in the world. In ten short years she'd progressed from innocent fool to prostitute.

Lanni tossed the keys and the money across the table to Don. "Get rid of the car, Don. I never want to see it again." And that went double for Chandler Scott.

13

HE WAS A BASTARD—an insufferable, unmitigated bastard. There was no other way to describe him. Lanni spent two weeks searching for a better word before she finally gave up and settled on that one.

It would have been bad enough if this were the first time he'd ever done this to her. But for it to be a repeat performance, and for him to be perfectly aware of the devastating effect he'd had on her ten years ago...well, there was just no excuse for the man. If thoughts could kill, there would have been one dead Don Juan in Texas.

On the other hand, Lanni supposed she had asked for what she got. She'd actually told him he didn't have to love her, that she just wanted him to accept her love. And she guessed that was what he'd done. But she hadn't expected him to be satisfied with a one-night stand.

Lanni covered very well. She laughed and kidded around with the staff as she always had, but she found that her throat hurt most of the time, as though she were constantly swallowing tears. She had to force herself to go on the next trip to the movies in Pentwater because just the sight of the camp garbage truck depressed her. Her favorite distraction was a long walk on the beach after dark, especially in the rain, which suited her inner mood.

Don treated her with kid gloves, never mentioning Chandler unless he had to. She supposed he knew her well enough to have guessed that all had not ended amicably between her and the Scott heir. Her defiant gesture with the car keys had probably been rather childishly transparent.

Teddy saw through her, too. After an initial period of reluctance to face his friends, the young man actually seemed more at peace than anyone had expected. He attended twice-weekly sessions with a psychiatrist in Muskegon—arranged by the absent Mr. Scott—and apparently in so doing began to learn a lot about himself.

One evening after supper, Teddy remained at the table with Lanni until everyone else had gone. She thought he needed to talk about his problems, but he surprised her. "You know, you're pulling one of my old tricks." At her quizzical look, he nodded hesitantly. "Whenever something hurts me, I always talk a lot to cover up. The more I hurt, the louder I laugh." He shrugged awkwardly. "It's funny that I can see it when you do it, but I couldn't see it in myself."

Lanni stiffened. "You think I'm hurting about something?"

His apologetic nod reminded her that he'd always tried to please everyone. Suddenly she knew this conversation required a great deal of courage on his part, and that Teddy was making the effort because he cared about her. She inhaled shakily. "You're right. I've been feeling like a total fool lately. But I'll get over it." Eventually. In another ten years or so.

"Didn't things work out with you and Chandler?"

"No."

He stared down at the table. "I'm sorry, Lanni. I wish they had."

"You like him a lot," she said softly.

"He's the only one who ever really understood about my father."

Lanni pondered that comment after Teddy left the eating lodge. Finally she concluded that it was just one more piece of the Chandler Scott puzzle that she would never be able to solve. And damn it all, she still *wanted* to.

ON HIS RETURN from Michigan, Chandler wasn't fit to be around. He was alternately preoccupied and short tempered, depressed and downright rude. His employees at Solo Enterprises discussed that fact behind his back and then elected one unlucky spokesperson to point it out to him—presumably the one best able to duck and run if Chandler took it wrong.

"Is it a woman, boss?" Max Kowalski asked him over a cup of coffee at the building site of the new mall in Richardson. Their friendship went back a long way and, Max hoped, could withstand a lot.

"Is what a woman?" Chandler responded absently, his eyes focused off in the distance. His thoughts were even farther away and not very pleasant. He still couldn't quite believe he'd walked out on Lanni like that, no matter how many times he told himself it was the only thing he could have done. She was bound to hate him now. That had been his intention, he conceded, but it was still hard to live with.

"This thing that's got you acting like a stuck pig."

"What?" Chandler swung around to look at his construction foreman with astonishment. "Who's acting like a stuck pig?"

Max was nodding sagely. "You are. Like a wounded bear. Like a jackass with a burr under its saddle. Like . . . like . . ."

"I get the picture," Chandler snapped, crushing his empty Styrofoam cup in one large fist and tossing it into the full-to-overflowing trash barrel nearby. It bounced off the contents of the large drum and landed at his feet again. Chandler glared down at the offending object as if it were responsible for the icy pain in his heart. "Call Hank and get these trash cans dumped," he ordered Max tightly. "*Now!*"

When he headed for his pickup truck, Max followed at a safe distance. "Well, Chandler? *Is* it a woman?"

Chandler didn't bother to look at his friend as he climbed in the cab. "Go to hell, Kowalski," he muttered succinctly.

Driving back to the Mesquite office, he decided maybe he needed to get away for a few days. It was time he had that talk with Guy Mitchell that he'd been dreading, and it wouldn't hurt to check on Caroline again.

LANNI'S EYES wandered affectionately over the rustic buildings in the camp compound, the arts and crafts shed, the library, the eating lodge and administration offices, the dormitory for visitors. The huge shade trees and the crisp Michigan air and especially the campers and staff were so firmly imprinted in her mind that she would never forget the place. She would miss it more than any other constant in her life. But her mind was made up.

"I thought you should know now," she told Don, who sat beside her on the bench outside the linen room. "Maybe there's someone on the staff that you'd want to hire to supervise next summer, since I'm resigning."

Don regarded her in silence for a while before he finally spoke. "If you're doing this to avoid seeing Chandler again, you don't have to worry. I'm beginning to doubt if he'll ever come back."

She didn't say anything. He probably wouldn't believe her if she denied his perception. Besides, she tended to cry these days without any provocation at all, and talking about Chandler definitely fell into the category of provocation.

After a moment Don sighed. "I'll miss you. Camp Ottawa won't be the same."

"Please." She forced a smile. "Don't get maudlin on me unless you're armed with a dozen handkerchiefs. Anyway, it's not quite August. I'll be here another month."

Don looked then as if he wanted to say something, but he just pursed his lips and nodded. She was glad he didn't try to play peacemaker.

Two hours later she feared he'd changed his mind. While she was helping the linen crew sort and fold clean sheets, Jack Mills stuck his head in the door of the linen room. "Don would like to see you in his office right away, Lanni."

She had a sneaking hunch it was about Chandler. When she saw the unfamiliar black Lincoln parked outside the administration building, her hunch solidified into conviction and her heart sank to her toes. *Please, God, don't let it be Chandler,* she prayed as she opened the door and went inside.

Chandler was nowhere to be seen. Neither was Don. Instead, an attractive blond woman in a blue linen dress stood at the window, gazing out past the wooded dunes to the tennis courts on the beach.

At the sound of the door closing, the woman turned with a warm smile, and Lanni recognized Caroline Scott. "Lanni, hello! How good to see you!"

"Hello, Mrs. Scott," she said, glancing around cautiously.

"I thought we had agreed that you were going to call me Caroline." Chandler's mother came forward and took Lanni's hand, then hugged her quickly. "You can stop worrying. I came by myself."

That relieved most of Lanni's apprehension, but not all. "This is certainly a surprise. Did you decide to spend some time at the cottage?"

"No, I'm just here for the afternoon once again." She hesitated. "Actually I came to talk to you."

"Me!" Lanni's eyebrows rose. "What about, Caroline?"

"About my son." While Lanni absorbed that disturbing news, the older woman looked around the office as if just now noticing the businesslike atmosphere. "Do you suppose we could go to the dining hall and have a cup of tea in privacy? Don kindly loaned me this office for our little chat, but somehow it's too . . . too impersonal, I think."

Too impersonal for what, Lanni wondered, growing more alarmed by the minute. But as she genuinely liked this woman, Lanni led the way to the kitchen and brewed them each a cup of tea, then settled Caroline at one of the clean tables in the empty dining room. She sat down across from the widow and folded her hands in her lap. "What was it you wanted to tell me about Chandler?"

Watching Caroline lift the thick white mug to take a sip of tea, Lanni had to admire the touch of elegance that the woman lent to the gesture, to the entire room. But her hand was trembling, Lanni saw. Caroline Scott was nervous about this so-called little chat! She put the cup down and met Lanni's eyes bravely. "I have to know if you're in love with him."

Lanni drew a deep, shaky, resentful breath. So much for Chandler's assertion that his mother liked Lanni. "You don't need to bother warning me off, Caroline. He isn't going to marry me."

"I'm not warning you off, and I'm not asking what he intends to do about you. I want to know if you love my son as much as I suspected that day at the cottage."

Caroline spoke calmly, reasonably, but Lanni wasn't pacified. "I don't mean to be rude, but this isn't really any of your business, is it?"

Lovely blue eyes looked straight into gray ones, and the regal chin tilted up. "Maybe not. But one day, when you have a child you love more than life itself and you see that child throwing away his best chance for happiness because he's proud and stubborn and utterly wrong about his own worth, then perhaps you'll understand why I'm asking, and why I'm going to persist until you answer me. Do you love Chandler?"

Lanni had absolutely no idea what Caroline was talking about, but she heard the underlying desperation in her voice and knew she had to be honest. She inclined her head once. "Yes. But he doesn't feel the same about me."

"So you think," Caroline murmured enigmatically, a trace of relief in her faint smile. The smile vanished as abruptly as it had come, and she leaned forward. "Tell me, Lanni, if Chandler didn't have a penny, would you still love him?"

Outraged color suffused Lanni's cheeks and she jumped to her feet. "I hope I didn't hear you correctly."

Chuckling warmly, the other woman waved her back into her seat. "Your face gives me the answer to that question. But I had to ask, Lanni. Chandler has a problem with his money, you see."

"You mean he's having financial difficulties?"

"No, I mean he has trouble believing people could possibly value him for himself rather than for his monetary wealth."

Lanni shook her head. "Doesn't he realize how many things there are about him to value? So much more than his money!"

"No, I'm afraid he doesn't know that. When I see how hard he can be on himself, denying himself the things he wants most of out life, I fear he must actually hate himself." The blue eyes filled with tears, and Caroline absently brushed them away. "It breaks my heart to think that I've failed him so terribly, Lanni. All his life he's been such a joy—a dear, precious son to my husband and me; a loving and protective big brother to Scotty—and now he's so totally alone!"

"Maybe he's alone because he prefers it that way," Lanni suggested huskily.

"No." Caroline shook her head and wiped her eyes again, her face reflecting sorrow. "No, Chandler needs love. He *wants* love. And he has so much love to give, if he would only stop punishing himself."

"Punishing himself for what?"

His mother studied Lanni at length. "Do you really care? Does it matter to you why he will never allow himself the privilege of marrying and having children of his own?"

Although she mulled over Caroline's question, she already knew the answer. "I care," she said after a moment. "Tell me why he's punishing himself."

Caroline reached for Lanni's hand and squeezed it, her eyes still damp. "That's something Chandler will have to answer. I can only tell you that he's tortured himself for ten years over this, keeping himself alone and far away from the ones who love him best despite everything my husband and I did to bring him back to us. It's a poison that is slowly killing his soul, and I can't save him. Leaving you here when he loves you was just more torture, self-inflicted and brutal."

None of this made any sense, especially the last part. "You think he loves me? You really think that?"

"My dear, I know he does. I saw him yesterday. He's lost weight, he doesn't sleep. He's a certified mess, and it's all because he doesn't think he's good enough for you." Her direct gaze made it impossible for Lanni to look away. "Will you go see him, Lanni? Make him talk to you?"

"I don't know. He may not tell me the truth. It may not do any good." But even as she spoke, Lanni knew she had to try, at least. She swallowed, then nodded. "All right, Caroline. I'll go."

LANNI RENTED A CAR at the Dallas-Fort Worth Airport and followed the directions Caroline had carefully written down. It took her over an hour to reach Chandler's farmhouse in the verdant, rolling countryside south of Dallas, and then, as she should have expected, he wasn't at home. Considering that it was Friday morning, she should have known he would be at work.

"So, Caroline, where do we go from here?" Lanni addressed the question to the air, standing on the front porch of the big, old, two-storied Victorian house and looking around at the clipped green lawn.

An enormous oak tree, at least two hundred years old, shaded the yard, and beds of blooming geraniums skirted the house, which was freshly painted white with green trim. From the stone water well in the side yard to the split-rail fence enclosing the acreage, the place was authentic turn-of-the-century Americana. There was no television antenna or satellite dish, no swimming pool, no trappings of wealth or modern luxury. . . just a lovely, secluded retreat.

She supposed she could always plant herself on that comfortable-looking porch swing over there and relax in the cool breeze until Chandler got home that evening. But what if he didn't come home? Besides, she knew what Caroline would think about such procrastination. Caroline would want her to track Chandler down and get on with the mission.

Mission impossible, Lanni thought as she climbed back in the car and headed once more toward the main highway to Dallas. She feared Caroline had been overly optimistic in thinking her dark, brooding son really gave a hoot about Lanni Preston. Just as she'd been so sure Lanni would find him at home that she hadn't suggested any other place to look.

She pulled the car over to the side of the road and tried to remember some clue that would help her locate him. He was a land developer, Don had said. In Mesquite. Suddenly she recalled the deposit slip with Chandler's note on the back. She had stuck it in her billfold.

Luckily it was still there. Holding it up triumphantly, Lanni congratulated herself on her disorganization. She'd known some good would eventually come of never throwing anything away.

Finding Solo Enterprises proved simple. Finding its owner didn't. The receptionist, a young black woman with an attractive smile, looked Lanni over with a great deal of interest and told her Mr. Scott hadn't been in yet that morning but that he had called in several times.

"Go back to the switchboard and talk to our dispatcher. Chandler usually tells Bert where he can be reached." She pointed to an office down the hall.

Bert was a surprise. Small and wispy, she looked as if a strong breeze would blow her away. She had to be seventy-five years old if she was a day. The minute she heard who Lanni was hunting, she put down her Spiderman comic book and got on the phone to trace Chandler's whereabouts.

"First time he rang up, he was at the library project in Irving," she explained between calls. "Next time he was on the freeway heading for Richardson. Some snag'd come up and he wanted me to have the architect meet him there at ten. They may be through by now. You don't talk like a Texan, honey. Did you say you live in Michigan?"

"I didn't say. Actually I live in St. Louis."

"Oh." Bert looked disappointed. She turned back to the instrument and punched in another number. "Wonder where that toot can be." She reached another construction crew and determined that the boss wasn't at the Arlington apartment-complex site, either. "So how was the weather in St. Louis when you took off this morning?"

"I didn't take off from St. Louis," Lanni said uncomfortably. "My flight left from Muskegon. I work up there at a summer camp."

Bert's eyes brightened. "Michigan! I knew it!" She clapped her hands and cackled in delight.

Two minutes later the object of her search called to ask if there was anything he needed to take care of on his way back to the office. With an expression of complete innocence, Bert handed Chandler a line about a potential client wanting to meet him for lunch at the local El Chico in half an hour. "I didn't write down her name, but she'll wait for you inside. You can't miss her."

Lanni stared at Bert in surprise when the older woman had hung up. "Bert, I didn't say I was a potential client. What made you tell him that?"

"Sheer genius, I guess." Bert looked vastly pleased with herself. "You never told me exactly what you wanted to see him about, but I can guess, you being from Michigan and all. Since he came back last month, that man ain't been the same person who took me off the welfare rolls and gave me this job. He's kind of wandering around in a fog, when he's not growling and snapping at everyone in sight."

And when Lanni shook her head, not wanting to think about how Chandler was going to react to seeing her, Bert added, "Would you rather talk to him here, with me and Rachel listening in at the door?"

Lord, no!

Thirty-five minutes later Lanni stood nervously in the foyer of the Mexican restaurant, practicing what she would say to him and wondering if she looked all right. She'd French-braided her long hair, leaving a few fluffy tendrils curling at the temples, and wore her favorite shirtdress, a white woven cotton with flared skirt and roll-back dolman sleeves. Her wide pink leather belt matched her low-heeled pumps, and she wore gold loop earrings and a gold bracelet. Despite the August heat, she thought she looked fairly cool and calm.

And then the door opened and closed and Chandler was there, and everything Lanni had planned to say departed from her brain without warning. He was so incredibly beautiful, so big and dark and handsome! He paused just inside the door with his chin tipped up, rolling his head from side to side in order to loosen the kinked muscles of his neck. His wide shoulders strained against the blue oxford cloth of his shirt, and the crisp khaki pants molded close to his long, impressive legs.

After a moment he lowered his head and looked around. His eyes skidded to a halt when they reached

Lanni, and he rubbed his hand over them quickly as if
to erase what he hoped was an apparition.

When he dropped his hand and looked back across
the dim entryway, she could see that his facial muscles
were tight, strained. She gave him a cautious little
smile. "Hello, Chandler."

His heart slowly sank to his knees. Heaven help him,
what was she doing there? She was beautiful, soft, fresh
looking, tempting. He wanted to touch her. He wanted
to turn around and walk back out the door. "Are you
supposed to be my potential client?"

"I guess so."

"Clever." His voice held no inflection.

"Bert thought so. I suppose she figured you wouldn't
come if you knew I'd be here."

"You told Bert about . . . what happened?"

Lanni gave a small, unamused laugh. "Hardly! Do
you honestly believe I'd brag about something like that?
I think Bert has some romantic notion about you and
me. So does Caroline, for that matter."

The hostess appeared just then and greeted Chandler by name, asking if he was expecting anyone else to
join them. He shook his head and followed Lanni and
the woman to a secluded corner booth, about as cheer-
ful as if he were being led to the gallows.

When they had been left alone with menus and a
straight bourbon for Chandler, he took a gulp of his
drink and then looked across the table at Lanni.
"What's this about Caroline?"

In the candlelit dimness it was hard to be sure, but she
thought Chandler really did look bad. His face seemed
almost gaunt, his eyes circled by dark smudges. She
wished she could reach out and touch him, but he didn't

look very approachable. "She came to see me. We had a talk about you."

He set his whiskey glass down with a clink, black eyes glittering. "No. She wouldn't."

"She did. She was worried about you."

"Why would she come to you?"

Lanni tried not to feel insulted at his question. Tears pricked her eyes, but she just smiled. "I told you, she has this crazy idea that you're pining away down here for love of me. I can see where she might worry. You look awful. But don't ask me why she thinks I'm responsible."

Chandler knew exactly why Caroline thought that. Because she knew all his secrets, including how he felt about Lanni.

His chest felt as though it were locked in a vise and someone was turning the screws. His head pounded, and a red haze clouded his vision. "You just couldn't take no for an answer, could you?" he asked with quiet fury. "You had to satisfy your curiosity. Well, did it work? Did you get so chummy with Caroline that she told you all the family dirt?"

Lanni watched him silently, not bothering to respond to his ridiculous accusations. All she could think of was his mother's assertion that Chandler was trapped in a cycle of hurting himself over something from his past.

He sat back, both hands clutched around his glass, his mouth grim. "Beautiful story, isn't it? I'm surprised you came all this way to see me after hearing the truth. Did you just want to tell me to my face what you think of me for pretending to be someone I'm not?" He tossed off his drink and stared at her with defiance in his dark eyes. "So tell me, Lanni, what did you find most enter-taining? The part where the girl stuffs her newborn baby in the service station trash can and hopes he'll die before anyone finds him? Or where she tries to black-mail the kid's father, only he runs her down in a car in-stead and kills her? It has potential, don't you think? Someone could probably write a trashy TV script about the sterling character of my parents."

"Your . . . parents?"

He saw her confusion and knew suddenly that she had no idea what he was talking about. Caroline hadn't told her. Of course not. She would have left that up to him. And he'd blown it.

Pain knotted his stomach and made him wish he had a whole bottle of bourbon to soothe it. "My parents, Lanni. A migrant fruit picker and a sleazy drug dealer. Didn't you ever wonder why I'm so dark when every-one else in my family had blond hair and blue eyes? Well, now you know. And if you're shocked, just im-agine how I felt when Chandler and Caroline had to tell me why my kidney wouldn't help Scotty. I wasn't his brother. I was just some half-breed kid whose mother had thrown him away."

The waitress came just then to take their order, but Chandler didn't even notice her. He stood up and stared down at Lanni with that burning rage that she knew now was directed inside himself. "You called it right the first time. I'm a bastard in every sense of the word. Just consider yourself lucky to be rid of me."

Before Lanni could open her mouth, he turned and walked out of the restaurant.

CHANDLER PARKED in front of the detached garage at his farmhouse and went slowly inside. He looked around the spacious kitchen vaguely before deciding that he wasn't hungry. A drink. That was what he needed. Something strong. Maybe if he passed out he could forget the encounter with Lanni.

After unplugging the phones, he fixed himself a Scotch and lay down across his bed to sip it and wait for it to take effect. Ten minutes later he tipped the glass up and drained it, thinking that something wasn't working right. Rather than ease his misery, the alcohol only seemed to be making him remember.

I didn't touch her, he thought with an ache of regret building in his chest. She had been right there, just inches away, and he hadn't put his hand on that satin skin or fingered the silky softness of her hair, hadn't caressed her cheek or cupped the fullness of her perfect breast in his palm. And now he would never again have the chance.

He hadn't apologized, either, for leaving her at the motel in Muskegon without saying goodbye. She would never know how hard that had been—how much it seemed like cutting out his heart and leaving it behind.

And he hadn't told her he loved her.

If he had it to do over again, he would make up for all those lost opportunities. He would forget about tomorrow and touch her in ways and places he'd dreamed about, and his touch would show her he was sorry for hurting her. But he would use real words to tell her he loved her, so she would be sure of it. If she were right there, right now, he would stroke her full bottom lip with the pad of his thumb, look into those soft gray eyes and say it: "I love you, Lanni Preston."

Talking to yourself now, he thought. *You're in bad shape.* He levered himself up and off the bed and wandered back in the direction of the bottle. Halfway there, he heard a sharp, steady knocking at the front door.

Figuring it was a salesman, he ignored it. After a few minutes, the pounding stopped. By that time, Chandler had downed his second drink—third, he amended, counting the one at the restaurant—and poured himself another and was sprawled across his bed again, telling the ceiling what he would say to Lanni Preston if she were there. "I'd look her right in the eyes and tell her I love her too much to walk away from her again. I'd ask her if she could forget who I am, or rather who I'm not, and just love me—"

"Yes," a familiar voice answered clearly, nearly causing Chandler's heart to stop beating.

When he felt the glass being removed from his slack fingers he focused on the vision that suddenly appeared above him. Lanni. Beautiful, warm, touchable Lanni, wearing that same white dress she'd had on at El Chico and looking virginal and sexy at the same time. She put his drink on the roll-top desk against the wall and returned to sit on the side of the bed.

He inhaled her fragrance and groaned. "What are you doing here, Lanni?"

Leaning down, she slid her fingers into his thick dark hair and smoothed it back from his temple, then curved her palm against his cheek. "I'm getting ready to have a long talk with the man I love."

He moved his head as if to draw back from her. "Don't say that. You can't love me."

"Why not?"

"Didn't you hear what I told you at the restaurant about my background? Not the unblemished family history the Scotts let me use, but the truth."

"Your background doesn't worry me."

He scowled. "Don't be so damned quixotic, Lanni. What do you know about me? What do *I* know? Nothing that would recommend me as a husband. My genes are probably so bad that I'll end up in a mental ward or on skid row by the time I'm forty."

"I don't believe that, and neither do you."

"I don't want to believe it," he agreed, his throat tight. "But you could never be sure. You'd always have to wonder when I'd start using drugs or drinking too much."

"Don't you think you've already had too much to drink? You're talking crazy."

Closing his eyes, he shook his head. "I haven't had enough. I thought the Scotch would help me forget you. Forget us."

Lanni saw tears form on his silky black lashes and kissed them away. "Why did you want to forget?"

He lay unmoving, mesmerized by the feel of her lips. "Because it hurts so much. I keep picturing your face when you discover who my parents were."

"You already described your parents pretty graphically, Chandler, remember? A fruit picker and a drug dealer, I believe you said." When he opened his eyes and searched her face, she met his gaze calmly. "It doesn't matter to me, you know."

His hands slid around her waist and locked behind her, and he pulled her down on top of him, burying his face against her breasts. He gave a rather choked laugh. "I had a feeling you might not be very objective about this. It's risky to love me, Lanni. You need someone to protect you from your own generous nature."

She rubbed her cheek against the top of his head. "And you plan to protect me?"

"Someone has to."

"Oh, yeah? Because of that so-called truth you keep talking about? What is the truth?" He pushed her away to give her a reproachful look, apparently thinking she was being flippant. "I mean it, Chandler. Are you sure you know the true story?"

"I know Caroline and Chandler wouldn't have lied to me about it. They hid it from me as long as possible, but when they finally had no choice, they told me the truth. And believe me, Lanni you don't want to hear this. It's a long, ugly story."

"I have plenty of time." She stood up and walked around the bed, kicked off her shoes, then stretched out there, propped up on one elbow so she could look down into his face.

Pain glittered in his eyes. "I've never told anyone before."

Reaching over, she laid her hand flat on his chest, over his pounding heart. Her expression was serene. "Chandler, if it will bother you, don't tell me. I know everything I need to know about you."

He shook his head roughly. "You don't! This isn't something you can shrug off." He released his breath in an impatient sigh. "All right, I'll tell you." He sat up and swung his legs off the bed, then sat there with his broad back to her, talking to the empty rocking chair in the corner. "You once said I thought I could get anything I wanted because I was Chandler Scott. You called me a rich, spoiled bastard, and you were right. Growing up, I took it all for granted—the good family, the respected name, the sense of being special. Deep down inside, I thought I was better than other people. The fact that there were hungry people living nearby didn't bother me. I never thought about what it might be like to be a migrant worker, following the fruit crops, hampered by a language barrier and a lack of education and job skills. The problems of other people had no relation to me."

He braced his hands on his knees and bent his head to stare down at the floor. "The worst thing that ever happened to me was my brother's illness. I refused to believe that he might die. When I found out he needed a kidney transplant, I couldn't understand why Mom and Dad wouldn't consider letting me give him one of my kidneys. I was healthy; we were brothers. But they wouldn't even let me undergo the tests to see if our tissue types were compatible." His voice dropped. "They didn't want to risk having me discover I wasn't their natural son."

Easing over onto his side of the bed, Lanni placed her hand on his rigid back, then began stroking. "What made them tell you?"

"When Dad called me home from camp that night ten years ago and I saw that Scotty was really going to die, I threatened to make the arrangements myself for the kidney transplant. At that point my parents had no choice but to tell me I'd been adopted."

She felt him shudder. "Lord, Chandler, that must have been a hard way to discover it."

He half turned to look at her, and she saw a decade of misery in his face. "This probably sounds obtuse, considering the way I look, but I'd never suspected they weren't my real parents. I was so arrogant, so totally sure of who I was. They'd always treated Scotty and me just alike. Hell, I was named after Chandler, Sr.!" Shaking his head, he turned away again. "Before the news had even begun to sink in, Scotty died, and in the middle of all the pain of losing him, I made them tell me about my adoption. They begged me to let it go, but I wouldn't, even though I could see that it tore them both apart to talk about it. I insisted on hearing every last revolting detail."

She could imagine how crazed with grief he must have been. "I'm sure they understood that you were hurting badly."

He stood up abruptly and strode across to the window. "Don't make excuses for me, Lanni. I acted like the son of a bitch that I was."

"Chandler, don't say things like that!"

"Why not? I found out that they had kept my adoption a deep, dark secret for one reason only: so I'd never have to know that my real mother hadn't wanted me—that she'd left me to die when I was just a few hours old. Then she'd tried to threaten the man who supposedly fathered me, to make him give her money, only his moral standards were no better than hers. He killed her and went to prison for it where he died a year later, stabbed to death by another inmate."

As she listened, Lanni's eyes filled with tears. It was impossible for her to conceive of anyone not adoring that black-eyed little cherub whose pictures Caroline had shown her. What if he had died? She jumped off the bed and ran across the room to throw her arms around Chandler. "I'm so sorry they hurt you," she whispered against his chest. "But I'm glad you had Caroline and your father and Scotty to love you all those years! How did they luck out?"

His arms had closed around her in automatic response to her embrace, and now his brow knit. Even knowing how sweet and loving she was, he found it hard to understand the way she was taking his disclosure. He'd expected at least a trace of horror and disgust. "Luck out?" he repeated quizzically.

Nodding, she hugged him tighter and lifted her tear-stained face. "I mean, how did they happen to adopt you?"

She thought that made them lucky? His chest constricted with a hope that he didn't dare acknowledge. "They were staying a few days at the cottage that September, after camp closed. Caroline read in the newspaper about a newborn infant being found near Grand

Rapids . . . about its mother being run down by a car a few hours later. The police had pieced the story together, and it was clear no relatives were going to claim the baby. Although she and my father had been married ten years and wanted children badly, she hadn't been able to have one. The minute she read that story, she sent Dad to get me. He said . . . he said she told him to pull whatever strings it took to make it legal and not to come back without me." Chandler looked down at Lanni and swallowed hard. "I never thanked him for succeeding."

"I'm sure he had his thanks, Chandler," she said, thinking of the affection she'd seen in all those family snapshots.

"I hope so. It must have cost him a lot to keep anyone from finding out who adopted me. The press had been having a field day with all the sordid details of the infant-found-in-trash-can story. I know, because ten years ago I went to the library and looked it up." He compressed his lips. "I can see now that they wouldn't have minded the publicity for themselves, but they hoped I'd never have to know about my parents."

Lanni was beginning to see a lot, too. Now it made sense why Chandler had reached out to Teddy with such compassion, and why he felt such rage over unfit parents. She understood his refusal to talk about his family—because he felt like an imposter. But some things still puzzled her. "Were the Scotts the only ones who knew your story, Chandler? How did they explain the sudden addition of a baby to the family?"

He released her and walked over to the window, rubbing the back of his neck with one hand. "I'm sure they sweated over that one before they came up with a plausible answer. They happened to be resting up at camp after nearly a year in Europe. Friends and business associates were told I had been born in Venice and that Mom and Dad hadn't mentioned her pregnancy to anyone because they feared she would miscarry, as she had done several times previously." He turned to watch Lanni move over to sit on the edge of the bed.

Crossing his arms on his chest, he leaned one shoulder against the old-fashioned highboy. "Their lawyer had to know the truth, and the judge who presided, and the social services agencies involved, but all the records were destroyed by court order." He shrugged. "Just one more advantage of having friends in high places."

"Sounds as if fate worked in their favor."

"It usually does for people who have money," he said cynically. "When Scotty was born two years later, Mom and Dad thought they had it all. I thought so, too. If Scotty had lived, maybe I'd still think that."

Yes, she guessed he probably would. "Chandler, I'm really sorry about Scotty, but . . . I think you're better off now than you were back then." She paused, seeking the right words, but he straightened and spoke before she could find them.

"Would you like a drink before you leave?"

She looked surprised. "Am I leaving?"

"You know the complete story now. What else is there to say?"

Her lips twitched. "You had something you wanted to say to me before you knew I was here. Shall I refresh your memory?"

"I had too much to drink. I never really intended to say that."

"Why? Because you're a coward?"

He glared. She was smiling sweetly, gray eyes laughing, head tipped to one side, an enchanting nymph whose saucy pose dared him to come closer.

"Or are you going to pretend you didn't mean it?"

"Lanni . . ." He stopped, his throat hurting too much to go on.

"You love me, Chandler, so don't bother denying it."

He lifted a hand toward her, then dropped it. "All right." He sounded tired, dejected. "I love you. And I'm sorry for running out on you in Michigan."

"The first time or the second?"

"Both times," he said harshly. "I won't do it again."

"You're darn right. I'm not going to give you the chance."

He nodded, knowing he didn't deserve her forgiveness.

"In fact," she said, her voice a sexy purr, "I may never again turn my back on you after we make love. That's a nasty habit you have of disappearing."

Anguish twisted in his gut. "Lanni, don't pretend that we have a future. You know the truth about me now, so why don't you just go on back to camp?"

Unable to tease him when he was still in such pain, she dropped her provocative demeanor. "I didn't come here to uncover the truth about you. I came because I love you, and because I thought we did have a future. You haven't said anything today to change that."

"I told you . . . I can't let you risk loving me."

"Darling, you can't stop me from loving you." She sighed. "Chandler, the only thing that bothers me about your story is that you've suffered so much over it. I can guess how hard it's been for you. I've seen it every time anyone mentions family to you, but Caroline also told me how it was ten years ago, how you refused to let her and Chandler, Sr., help you. How you felt you had to get away from them completely, to make something of yourself, all by yourself. She didn't explain why, but I can see your reasons now. You had to establish your own identity. You felt you had something to prove."

She rose and went to him, put her hands on his shoulders and spoke fiercely. "Well, now you've proved it. You've made your own way with unquestionable success. You've got friends down here who wouldn't recognize the Chandler Scott I knew ten years ago. They'd say I was lying if I described him. That Chandler wasn't a real person, and I'm not just talking about knowing or not knowing his true identity. The thing is, nothing had touched that other Chandler. His life was too easy. But you—you're a man, not a spoiled kid. You feel—hurt, love, hope. That's why I love you more than I ever could have loved the person you were back then."

Her expression was tender, her words solemn and full of promise. Squeezing shut his eyes, he bent his head until his forehead touched Lanni's. "I hope to heaven you mean that."

"Of course I mean it! I'm not in the habit of making declarations of love lightly. Are you?"

"I'm not in the habit of making declarations of love, period. But I'll make an exception for you. I love you, lady. If I live to be a hundred, I won't be able to show you how much."

"Can't you at least try?"

He laughed shakily and lifted his head. "With pleasure." His voice was low, warm, soft as a caress. He tilted her face up, then covered her mouth with his in a kiss so beguiling, so subtly intoxicating, that she didn't realize what was happening to her until it was done. Her heart melted slowly and her knees turned to honey, causing her to sway against him and lean there, propped against his taut strength. His arms wrapped her up and pulled her to him, bringing their heated bodies into prolonged sensitized contact with each other.

She felt his lips move to the corner of her mouth, then down her neck, and she threw back her head to feel more. Thrilling jolts of energy shot like magic arrows through her inner being—charges of desire that sped up her pulse and pumped her blood faster and hotter.

While his mouth still nibbled hungrily, his hands groped to unbutton the front of her dress and skim it off her shoulders, down past her hips. The white cotton slithered into a pool at her feet, leaving her slender length bare except for a few bits of silk and nylon. Exercising all the restraint he could muster, he unfastened her bra and found the dusky-rose tip of a breast, then began rolling it between thumb and forefinger until it hardened with excitement.

"Ahh, Lanni," he moaned, his hands sliding down her ribs to her tiny waist. "I'd like to take this slow and easy, but you make it impossible." He pressed his face to her throat and inhaled, trembling with the force of his need. The most potent evidence of that need throbbed hot and strong against Lanni, feeding her own hunger.

"I know," she said with a wicked chuckle. "I'm not exactly in command of myself. Maybe we should just, mmm, go for it."

Chandler nodded his agreement, conceding that it was out of his hands. It had been from the first time he touched Lanni, six weeks ago at the cottage. He'd craved her with a deep, unrelenting passion ever since.

He quickly shed his own clothes and lay down upon the quilted coverlet, and his body and Lanni's came together swiftly, perfectly, as if magnetized in all the right places. Creamy skin molding to dark, hands both soothing and disturbing as they searched and found secret parts, the two of them synchronized their movements until they lost the last traces of conscious control and were drawn into a vortex of rapturous feelings. Spinning, spiraling emotions whirled them to the farthest reaches of the universe and back with an intensity that left them breathless.

For a long time afterward, unmindful of the tears of joy that glistened on her long lashes, Lanni clung to him. She kissed his bare damp chest, tasting his flesh and relishing his male scent, rubbing her lips against the crisp dusting of hair. "I may have to revise my opinion of you chairman-of-the-board types," she announced. "I used to think the only things you had going for you were your egos."

"And now?"

"Now I can see, mmm, other assets."

"Such as?"

She ran a hand down the flat plane of his belly, admiring his lean, dark good looks. He was everything she had ever wanted in a man. Eyes half-closed to hide their sparkle, she pretended to look him over assessingly. "Oh . . . such as . . . well, such as . . . stocks and bonds. I'll bet you have an impressive investment portfolio."

He grasped her by the waist and hauled her on top of him in mock outrage. "Stocks and bonds! I thought you loved me for myself."

"Oh, I do, I do." She shivered at the trail his fingertips were making along her spine as they worked at loosening her braid. Lazily his hands sifted through her hair, combing, smoothing. "I'd love you, Chandler Scott, even if your name was Clyde Clodhopper. Even if it was John Doe or Joe Blow."

"What if it was Miguel Garcia?"

She shifted just enough to kiss the bronze skin that covered his heart. "Then I'd want to be Mrs. Miguel Garcia. It doesn't matter to me what name you were born under. Just as Caroline loves you because you'll always be her son, not because she gave birth to you." Raising up a couple of inches, she grinned at him. "I have a terrific idea. You can teach our kids to speak Spanish." She laid her cheek back down. "After you teach me, that is."

He continued to stroke her with gently drifting hands. "Kids . . . you really want to take a chance on me as a father?"

"The only chance I'll be taking is that our children might end up looking like me. I want them all to have your hair, your eyes, your gorgeous olive skin. I'd like a dozen little angels just like you to love."

When he nosed into her tousled hair and she felt his wet cheek brush her throat, she rolled to one side in concern. "What's the matter, Chandler? You don't want a dozen kids? I was exaggerating. Six will suit me fine. Or three. I'll even settle for one and a half." She got up on one elbow to study his face and saw the tears welling in his eyes. "Just, please, Chandler, don't look at me like that! Don't you want children?"

He flung his forearm across his eyes for a moment, then drew a long deep breath and lowered his arm. He smiled at her with a brilliance that made the breath catch in her throat. "Lanni, I want *your* children. It's just that . . . Lord, for so long I've been certain I could never again be part of a family, and I'm having a little trouble getting used to the idea." His smile faded. "What do you think your parents will say?"

She traced her index finger down his handsome nose. "About what?"

"About me as a prospective husband for their only daughter."

"It doesn't matter what they say. Anyway, by the time we tell them, you should be more than a mere prospect, my darling. I wasn't planning to wait long to—how do they say it down here in Texas? Get hitched?"

Laughing, he nipped at her fingertip. "You know what else they say down here—'Northern broads sure are pushy!'"

"Guilty as charged." She leaned over and kissed him with tantalizing languor on the mouth, the throat, the collarbone, the shoulder. "Would you rather have a long engagement?"

The arousing fire of her lips heated his blood. "Does three days qualify as long? I might be able to hold out until Monday. If you'll stop tempting me, that is."

She sat up and raised both hands to indicate that she wouldn't dream of touching him again. "Hey, I can play fair. I'll even let you pick where we get married. Dallas? Philadelphia?"

She was beautiful, he thought. She looked like a fragile work of art in creamy gold porcelain, sitting crosslegged on the bed beside him, her silky chestnut hair draping over her shoulders, not quite hiding her nakedness. Lady Godiva. A lady, definitely.

Black eyes intent, he lay staring up at her. "I thought . . . maybe . . . the chapel at Camp Ottawa?"

Lanni adored the idea. "With Caroline and Don and Teddy and all the staff there! Perfect! And we can honeymoon at the cottage. There'll be so many things to do in Michigan—swimming and sailing and taking the Ludington ferry over to Wisconsin—"

"Oh, yeah, all kinds of things to keep us busy," he interrupted with a secretive little smile as he reached out and pulled a strand of her hair, watching it curl around the tip of his finger. "You'll have all those johns to clean and windows to wash."

"What!" she protested, trying to ignore his wandering hand.

He nodded. "And tables to set and linen to fold."

The slow rhythm of his hand stroking her hair and the soft flesh beneath almost hypnotized her. "I quit. I resign right now!" Hardly able to breathe, she moaned.

"Don't tell me you want me to spend our honeymoon scrubbing and polishing."

"No-o-o-o," he said, focusing on her soft pink mouth. "But I don't want to spend it swimming and taking ferry-boat rides, either. I thought we could pass the time doing something else. Something much more pleasurable and, mmm, mutually satisfying." His voice caressed her like a velvet kiss. "We won't even have to leave the house to enjoy this."

"Sounds promising," she whispered. "What did you have in mind?"

He took her in his arms and pulled her down to him, his eyes glowing with a look of ineffable love that was reflected in hers. "Why don't I show you?"

An hour later, the demonstration was still in progress.

Harlequin Temptation

COMING NEXT MONTH

ATTRACTIVE, SPACE SAVING BOOK RACK

Display your most prized novels on this handsome and sturdy book rack. The hand-rubbed walnut finish will blend into your library decor with quiet elegance, providing a practical organizer for your favorite hard-or soft-covered books.

Only $9.95

Approximately 16" x 8" when assembled

Assembles in seconds!

To order, rush your name, address and zip code, along with a check or money order for $10.70* ($9.95 plus 75¢ postage and handling) payable to *Harlequin Reader Service*:

Harlequin Reader Service
Book Rack Offer
901 Fuhrmann Blvd.
P.O. Box 1396
Buffalo, NY 14269-1396

Offer not available in Canada.

*New York and Iowa residents add appropriate sales tax.

BKR-1A

Harlequin Intrigue
Adopts a New Cover Story!

We are proud to present to you
the new Harlequin Intrigue cover design.

Look for two exciting new stories each month, which
mix a contemporary, sophisticated romance with the
surprising twists and turns of a puzzler . . . romance
with "something more."